"I want to look, not touch."

"B-but why?"

"I should have thought that was perfectly obvious," Marcus replied silkily. "You, Sheona, are about to become Shireen for a few days."

"No!" Sheona gasped, horrified. "No, no, no! I *hate* modeling."

"There's no choice. You'll have to stand in for Shireen until she turns up. Now, I need a good look at you."

"No," Sheona repeated, backing toward the door. "Never!"

"I can ruin your sister."

Sheona froze. Slowly, disbelievingly, she turned to him. "You wouldn't!"

"Advertising is a relentless and unforgiving business—and the law's the law. You can ruin your twin, or save her."

Anne Beaumont started out as a Jill-of-all-writing-trades, but she says it was her experience as a magazine fiction editor, buying stories and condensing them for serialization, that taught her to separate the bones of a story from the flesh. In her own writing, she starts with her characters—"a heroine I can identify with, then a hero who seems right for her." She says that many writers work in reverse—plot first, then characters. "That's fine," she says. "If we all had the same method, we might all be writing the same books, and what a crashing bore that would be!" In addition to Anne Beaumont's romance novels, the author has written historicals under the pen name Rosina Pyatt. She lives on the Isle of Wight, with its sparkling white beaches, and has three children, of whom she is immensely proud.

Books by Anne Beaumont

HARLEQUIN ROMANCE
3049—ANOTHER TIME, ANOTHER LOVE
3199—A CINDERELLA AFFAIR

HARLEQUIN PRESENTS
1231—THAT SPECIAL TOUCH
1391—SECRET WHISPERS

IMAGES OF DESIRE
Anne Beaumont

Harlequin Books

TORONTO • NEW YORK • LONDON
AMSTERDAM • PARIS • SYDNEY • HAMBURG
STOCKHOLM • ATHENS • TOKYO • MILAN
MADRID • WARSAW • BUDAPEST • AUCKLAND

Original hardcover edition published in 1992
by Mills & Boon Limited

ISBN 0-373-03241-2

Harlequin Romance first edition January 1993

IMAGES OF DESIRE

CHAPTER ONE

MARCUS DRUMMOND wasn't the easiest man in the world to contact. By the time Sheona Murray had talked her way past the switchboard operator, two secretaries and a personal assistant, she was fighting a nervous impulse to drop the telephone back in its cradle and try again later.

But her sister Shireen had been insistent. Drummond had to be told now, immediately. Later just wasn't good enough. If he chewed her up then what the hell, it was better over and done with. No sense in stewing about it all day. Especially as he couldn't reach out and damage her, not over the phone.

'Reach out and damage me?' Sheona had echoed. 'What sort of a man is he?'

'Very physical,' Shireen had replied, and growled deep in her throat.

Grief, Sheona had thought, but Shireen had only laughed and gone on gaily, 'Sorry to drop this in your lap, darling, but I know you'll come through for me, the same as I would for you. Plead, pacify, do whatever you have to, but get me a few extra days. I'll explain everything when I get back.'

'Get back from where?' Sheona had wailed, but the phone had gone dead.

It was clicking with life now as she waited for somebody to remember she was hanging on, and long distance, too!

Sheona tried to use the time to sort her thoughts into some kind of coherent order, but Shireen had hardly been coherent herself. She'd been excited, full of some big secret she wasn't ready to share, even with the sister who had to do her dirty work for her.

'Drummond.'

Sheona almost dropped the phone. The voice was so male, so abrupt that, although she'd been waiting interminably for the connection, she was caught unawares.

Marcus Drummond's voice was also discouraging, as though he resented being interrupted from something infinitely more important than talking to her. Suddenly she was very glad she was at the end of a line and not face to face with him.

'Very physical' her sister had said. Sheona could believe it.

'Mr Drummond,' she began nervously, 'I'm Sheona Murray, Shireen's sister——'

'I've been briefed that far, so please come to the point,' he broke in, and his 'please' did nothing to disguise his irritation.

Sheona, always sensitive to disapproval, lost track of what she'd been about to say and dried up. She felt an awful fool, and cursed her sister for thrusting her into such an awkward situation. Shireen, so outgoing, was incapable of understanding how a shy person could die a thousand deaths over something that seemed perfectly straightforward to her.

The phone line seemed to crackle with Marcus Drummond's impatience, and after a second or two he demanded, 'Shireen's not sick, is she?'

'N-no, nothing like that. It's just that—that——' Hell, this dreadful man was having such a shattering effect on her that she couldn't get the words out. She'd known it would be hard, but he was making it impossible.

A bully, she thought. And she loathed bullies.

'Miss Murray, I'm very pushed for time,' he snapped, and, whatever Shireen had said, Sheona did feel damaged, even over the phone. She crushed very easily, worse luck.

She swallowed nervously, then flinched as he prompted irascibly, 'I haven't got all day.'

Sheona panicked and her words came out in a blunt, undiplomatic rush. 'Shireen's abroad. She won't be back for a few days.'

'*What?*'

His rage, his disbelief, assaulted her ear with such violence that Sheona had to fight the urge to drop the phone like a red-hot coal. But she knew her sister wouldn't have chickened out if their situations had been reversed, and so she soldiered on valiantly, 'She's been unavoidably delayed. She says she'll join you on location a few days later than she's supposed to.'

'What does she mean by "a few days"?'

'I don't know,' Sheona confessed, feeling more threatened than ever. Marcus Drummond's voice had changed completely. It was calm, cold, and somehow twice as frightening. His rage had been a live thing, something tangible that could be fought, but now he sounded silky. Instinct told her he wasn't to be trusted when he was silky. She was sure it was a disguise for ruthlessness.

An icy shiver ran down her spine. Yet what could he do to her? She was innocent of any crime, and she didn't have to worry about Shireen. Her sister had been born knowing how to take care of herself, even against the Marcus Drummonds of this world. Not for the first time Sheona wished that she had that sort of confidence, too, then she wouldn't get so flustered, feel so inadequate, just because some unknown man was giving her a hard time.

'I'm sorry,' she mumbled.

'Is that supposed to make me feel better?' he asked with the same terrible silkiness. 'Do you know I have millions tied up in this campaign, and it's all built around your sister?'

'Millions,' she repeated, startled. 'No, I——'

'Well, you know now,' he broke in, his silkiness sliding into a snarl, 'and I'm not chucking those millions down the drain just because your sister has got too big for her boots. I need her tomorrow, as contracted. Where is she?'

The last bit, the question, had all the impact of a bullet. Sheona recoiled and faltered, 'I don't know...'

'Tell me, dammit!'

'I can't. All I know is that she phoned me a few minutes ago and asked me to let you know she'll be a few days late. Oh, and there was something about her suntan's OK so there's no need for topping-up time. She said that would make her late arrival all right.' Sheona paused, hoping that made more sense to him than it did to her.

There was an ominous silence, then he exploded, 'She knows better than that! What's she got, a spot on her nose or something?'

'Shireen never gets spots!' Sheona exclaimed. 'And if she did she wouldn't—wouldn't——'

'Break her contract?'

So it really was that bad, was it? Sheona had feared as much when Shireen had phoned her instead of Marcus Drummond direct. Her instinct to defend her sister remained, though, and so she suggested nervously, 'She's n-not breaking it exactly, is she? Just stretching it a little.'

'Don't play word-games with me, Miss Murray. A contract is kept or it is broken. It doesn't stretch! If you want to save your sister's skin you'll stop prevaricating and tell me where she's holed up—and with whom.'

Sheona's face flamed as her blood heated with disgust at his crudeness. 'There's no need to be offensive,' she retorted stiffly, 'and there's no point in going round in circles. I've told you all I know. I'm sorry if you've been inconvenienced, but you'll have to take it up with Shireen when she returns.'

'Whenever that might be!' he mocked. 'I'm afraid that's not good enough. I'm taking it up with you right here and now. Where are you? I presume you know that much.'

If Marcus Drummond could reduce her to a quivering wreck over the telephone there was no way she was going to let him get close to her. She might feel unsafe now, but that was just a nervous reaction to his long-distance bullying. In the same room with him would be something else again.

Gathering the tattered rags of her dignity about her, she replied frostily, 'I don't live in London and I couldn't help you if I did. I can only relay Shireen's apologies, and that will have to do until she can explain more fully herself. Goodbye, Mr Drummond.'

She dropped the receiver back into its cradle and stared at it as though she expected Marcus Drummond's voice to continue its assault on her in spite of the cut connection. She was almost surprised at the silence. Such was the force of the man that he still seemed to be with her. He felt as physical, as real as the furniture around her.

It took some time for his power to wane, for her limbs to stop trembling, for her to start feeling foolish that a voice on the telephone could have such a traumatic effect on her. Only then did she accept that the connection between herself and Marcus Drummond really had been cut, and there was nothing for her to fear.

Idiot! she told herself crossly. There never had been anything to fear! Except, perhaps, her own timidity. None of this would have happened if she'd stood up to her sister in the first place, insisted she did her own dirty work. But Shireen had always been the dominant sister, and old habits stuck.

Not for the first time, Sheona wished she hadn't been
born a twin. Still, she'd made the break for indepen-
dence quite a few years ago, and against all predictions
she'd succeeded in creating a separate existence for
herself. It was only when Shireen swept back into her
life that the old submissiveness made her half a person
again.

Sheona found herself frowning at her reflection in the
hall mirror above the elegant little console table that
supported the phone. Was she over-dramatising? No, she
didn't think so. She'd spent so much of her life feeling
like one half of a whole that it was fatally easy to slip
back into that mentality.

The puzzle was that Shireen had always been whole—
and then some! It was as though she'd had her whole
self and half of Sheona, too. Sometimes, like during her
hurried phone call this morning, she acted as though she
still did.

Somebody in the tiny hall was sighing, and, since
Sheona was the only one there, it had to be her. She
sighed again, not knowing what for, and took off the
glasses that were making her reflection fuzzy. She only
needed the glasses for close work, and she'd been doing
some very close work indeed when Shireen's call had
interrupted her.

She should be getting back to it, and yet she lingered,
searching the mirror for answers to questions it couldn't
give. Like why Shireen thrived on being the centre of
attention while she herself shrank from it...and why
Shireen had always been loved and spoiled while she
herself was dismissed as 'Oh, the other twin'. It really
didn't make a lot of sense, considering how alike they
looked—or had looked until she'd deliberately done all
she could to make herself different.

Nobody mistook her any longer for Shireen, the
famous model. She was indisputably Sheona, the non-

famous artist. It suited her. She liked being anonymous. It was so much better than being the barely tolerated 'other twin'.

So there was a certain satisfaction in seeing her unmade-up face reflected back at her. It had never really needed painting, anyway. Her brown eyes were large and lustrous, her complexion unblemished, her nose straight, her full lips firmly formed, her neck long and graceful, and her dark hair thick and wavy as it fell from the orange chiffon scarf that held it in a pony-tail.

Mirrored there was every detail that had made Shireen a top model—except for the intangibles, the main one being that the cameras loved Shireen. In her photographs she glowed with life and charisma. Sheona didn't glow with anything. She was just a flat reflection, a negative to Shireen's positive, and so she had broken away, fearing that if she didn't she would somehow be destroyed.

Heavy stuff, Sheona thought, an ironic smile curving her lips as she moved away from the mirror. Stuff I haven't bothered about for years. What had brought it on? Surely not that harassing exchange with Marcus Drummond?

Yes, definitely that exchange, she mused, swinging her glasses in her hand as she walked along the polished wooden boards of the narrow passage. The colourful, arty slip-mats she and her housemate had bought for the floor were now hanging on the walls—because they'd slipped too much. But Sheona didn't see them. She was still looking inward, reflecting on just how shattering that phone call had been to the serene existence she'd carefully created for herself.

Marcus Drummond wasn't to know it, of course, but briefly he'd swept her back into a world she'd never been able to cope with, peopled as it was with characters like him who'd had no time for the 'other twin'.

Not that any of them had been as blatant about it as he had! Oh, no! She'd had to endure politely restrained impatience, the soul-destroying feeling that she was in the way but had to be tolerated for fear of upsetting the twin who mattered.

Marcus Drummond, though, hadn't bothered with that kind of finesse, however false. He'd also had the nerve to imply that Shireen was spoilt! Whoever he was, Sheona couldn't recall a more blatant example of the pot calling the kettle black.

And yet . . . and yet . . . he was a man who generated a certain kind of excitement, even over a machine as impersonal as the telephone. Without actually having seen him, she knew there was nothing negative about him. He was chock-full of all those screaming positives that made her shrink into her shell and stay there until all danger was past.

Danger? Now she really was over-dramatising! If Drummond was still raising hell it was his staff who would have to endure it, and later Shireen if he hadn't calmed down by the time she re-surfaced.

As for herself, she was in the clear.

Funnily enough, it was with a strange sense of anti-climax rather than relief that Sheona settled down again at the workbench in her studio, indisputably her very favourite room. With its flagstoned floor, low beamed ceiling, and whitewashed walls, it had once been the scullery at the back of the narrow old house. She'd designed the conversion herself, adding extra windows to let in lots of good northern light so vital for her work, and to give her an intimate view of the small walled garden.

She was happy here, happier than she'd ever been in her life. She was doing work she loved, and she was blissfully free of the tension of having to compete with Shireen. It was a tension her sister had never known, and therefore never understood, any more than she'd understood why Sheona had chosen to come to this resort on the south coast when she'd graduated from college.

'Boring Bournemouth!' Shireen had exclaimed at the time. 'You must be mad! Why bury yourself in a place like that? London's where it's all happening, knucklehead!'

But Sheona hadn't listened. She'd known what she'd wanted, what was right for her. What was more, she'd never found Bournemouth boring. She loved the quiet winter months, when she built up her stock, as much as she loved the bustling summer months that brought extra customers for her hand-painted china. And, far from being buried, she'd continued the process of coming truly alive in her own right—a process she'd started when she'd parted ways with Shireen at sixteen to concentrate on her schooling as a preparation for art college.

Sheona picked up a fine-pointed chinagraph pencil to continue sketching the outline of a brown and white collie on to a bone-china plate. This was one of the special commissions that were rapidly becoming the most lucrative side of her business, and she worked from sketches and photographs she'd taken of the dog.

At least, she should have worked, but her concentration had gone. She found herself staring out at the fuchsias, roses and geraniums that still bloomed in hanging baskets and flowerbeds, although it was October. Autumn was being kind to the flowers this year, so unusually mild and sunny that the brilliant summer scarcely seemed to have ended.

Sheona shook her head to clear it of all the memories stirred up by her phone encounter with the world she'd abandoned. She waited for the customary tranquillity of her present life to overcome her like a soothing benediction, but nothing happened. Instead, her artist's mind was conjuring up an image of Marcus Drummond, and, since she only had his voice to go on, her imagination was running riot.

All the dark colours, she thought, to suggest the threatening power that had overcome her on the telephone. Black hair, black eyebrows, brown eyes. Then Sheona grimaced because, reduced to colours, that description could have passed for her own. So she gave Drummond a powerful frame, large strong hands, big shoulders and heavily muscled thighs—yes, definitely heavily muscled thighs.

Now why was she so sure about that? With an involuntary contraction of her own muscles she realised that the image she retained above all others of Marcus Drummond was one of undiluted sexuality. How strange…especially as she'd never gone for the caveman type herself. Avoided them like the plague, in fact, just as she avoided anything that made her feel threatened. It was all part of the safe haven she'd created for herself, a haven where her art could grow and to blazes with everything else.

But Marcus Drummond, having drawn his image on her mind, refused to go away, or even to be mocked away. Clear off, she told him. You're probably a flabby, sexless sixty-year-old who uses the telephone to project an image you wished you had.

Yet still he stayed with her, and still the chinagraph pencil stayed idle in her hand. In the end she flung it down in disgust and stood up. It was close enough to lunch. She might as well take a break, allow time for the hiccup in her normal routine to fall into perspective.

Usually she had a snack at home, but today she decided a walk would be likelier to clear her mind. She pulled her smock over her head, revealing the black jumper and stretch jeans beneath, changed her comfortable slippers for thonged sandals and headed back along the passage. She lifted a light anorak off the coat stand, slung it over her shoulder in case the weather cooled, then strode out into the quiet cul-de-sac lined on both sides with identical tall, narrow houses like the one she shared with Petra.

A few minutes' walk through the back streets, down a pedestrian-only shopping precinct almost as flower-filled as her garden, across a park in the city centre and up to another shopping precinct brought her to an old-fashioned pub where Petra often grabbed a snack at midday.

She went in and, although the pub was pretty full, Petra wasn't there. Sheona was sorry. A few minutes' conversation with her happy-go-lucky friend would certainly have ousted Drummond's image and put her back on even keel. Still, the relaxed atmosphere of the unpretentious pub with its ancient mirror-engraved walls and little iron-based wooden tables would probably do the trick.

There were still a few late holidaymakers about to mingle with the locals, and Sheona watched them as she lunched frugally on a cheese roll and half a pint of shandy. She'd been out of art college almost a year now, but she still retained her student ways, practising the delicate art of surviving on a small budget without precisely starving herself. Not that she had to manage on a grant any more. These days it was the mortgage she shared with Petra that ate up her earnings.

An idle half an hour later, Drummond was banished from Sheona's mind and she was happy again. She strolled back home and resumed her work, unbothered by outside distractions. By mid-afternoon not only was the collie's sketch done, but she'd completed other sketches as well in preparation for a painting session tomorrow.

The contentment that came from knowing she'd worked well made her feel good as she put down her

pencil and stretched. This was the life! The only pressure
she had to endure now was the pressure she put on
herself, and she thrived on that. There was a special thrill
in developing and stretching her talent, a deep satisfaction in knowing she could survive by herself. She
simply didn't need the hassle of her old life…the tension
of trying to please difficult people like Marcus
Drummond.

Blast! Now why had her mind shot back to him?

Her frown, and the quiet of the mellow old house,
was fragmented by a loud double knock on the front
door. Oh, no, she thought, not another double-glazing
salesman. She and Petra could barely afford the roof
over their heads, let alone expensive extras. The last of
their spare cash had gone on a studio for her and fitting
out a shop for Petra, and it had been scrape and pinch
for them both ever since.

Sighing, Sheona began the route march straight
through the house to the front door, and the harsh double
knock came again before she was halfway there. She was
annoyed. She also realised that salesmen never knocked
like that. Theirs was a polite request for attention, not
this demanding answer-or-else sort of summons.

She opened the door, fully prepared to tear a strip off
whoever was doing his or her damndest to knock the
door down, and then froze as an icy premonition struck
her. She actually felt her skin contract and the hairs rise
on the back of her neck in a primeval response to
threat…a threat posed by a big and powerful man.

It wasn't the fact that he was big and powerful that
drove the colour from her cheeks and the breath from
her lungs, though. It was because he was the living in-
carnation of the image Marcus Drummond had burned
into her brain. And that with only an inanimate tool like
a telephone to project his voice, his personality, his
virility!

Now he was here. Black hair, brown eyes, big shoulders, heavily muscled thighs—everything exact down to the last detail. Tell-tale colour crept back into Sheona's cheeks as she breathlessly picked up again on the sexual connotation of her preoccupation with his thighs.

But it couldn't be him! It simply couldn't be! Marcus Drummond belonged to Shireen's world, not hers. Besides, he didn't even know where she lived...

CHAPTER TWO

SHEONA could only believe that Marcus Drummond was a figment of her imagination, and that none of this was really happening. She just had to close her eyes to banish him back into her brain, hopefully never to escape again. His outline was muzzy, anyway. She'd forgotten to take off her glasses again. She reached up to remove them, then let her hand fall. In her panic they seemed to offer some kind of protection, and instinct told her she needed all the protection she could get if he was really there.

In the meantime, she blinked. Then she almost fainted as Marcus Drummond, larger than life and just as real, guessed her intention and mocked harshly, 'I'm Marcus Drummond all right, and it's no use trying to blink me away, Sheona Murray. You didn't think you could hide from me, did you?'

Then his dark eyes dropped from her bespectacled face to her smock and he groaned, 'Good lord, you're pregnant.'

'I'm not!' Sheona exclaimed fiercely, her face flaming for no good reason. 'This is an artist's smock. I don't see that it's any of your business, anyway.'

'You will.' He pushed past her, his arm brushing her shoulder as he made space for himself in the narrow passage.

Sheona resented the physical contact as much as she resented his intrusion into her home, and she exclaimed wrathfully, 'What do you think you're doing? Now just you listen to me——'

'You're the one who will be doing the listening,' he interrupted, and Sheona was so strung up by this time that she jumped in alarm when a gust of wind caught the front door and slammed it shut. The last thing she wanted was to be closed inside the house with this dreadful man, but before she could re-open it he began walking down the passage.

With an outraged, 'Hey!' she hurried after him, and almost collided with him as he stopped at the first door he came to. He opened it, stared in and closed it again.

Sheona began to feel flustered. That was the sitting-room but it was in an awful state, only half-stripped of its hideous old wallpaper and with tatty bits of curtaining protecting the oddments of furniture she and Petra had gathered together. He wasn't to know, naturally, that it was the condition of the house that had brought it down to their price-range, or that they were putting it right themselves in their spare time. What little spare time they had, that was.

'Mr Drummond,' she began indignantly, but she was brushed aside once more as he strode on and opened the next door. The dining-room . . . and, grief, looking at it through his eyes, she realised it was in a worse state than the sitting-room. Up until now familiarity had blunted its effect on her, but the paper was hanging away from the walls of its own accord, and the second-hand table and chairs looked awful as they waited to be stripped of chipped, discoloured paint.

If anybody else had been looking around uninvited she would have laughed and said it served them right, but Drummond just made her feel embarrassed. He was so immaculate himself in his expensive Italian shoes, tailored white shirt and beautifully cut Savile Row suit— and the very best of Savile Row at that!

He also made her painfully conscious of the limp chiffon tying back her hair, and the paint stains on her voluminous smock. Even her dark stretch jeans had picked up some dog hairs. She didn't have a dog, either. The hairs must have come from one of her canine subjects.

Sheona wished she could explain all this to Marcus Drummond. Then she was annoyed with herself because there was no reason in the world why she should justify herself to him. That still didn't stop her wanting to, even though she knew he wouldn't be the slightest bit interested. Contempt was written all over him, the arrogant brute.

Was that why she was feeling as she used to in the old days—way below Shireen's exalted status? Of course it was! Sheona hated what was happening to her, hated him for making it happen.

The next door he opened was the bathroom's, and at least she didn't have to blush for that. It was almost finished, with bright new wallpaper and just a few floor-tiles still waiting to be stuck in place. But what on earth was the man looking for? Did he think Shireen was hiding somewhere? He couldn't know too much about her sister, then. The only time Shireen came this far south was when she was flying over it on her way to Monaco or somewhere.

'If you've quite finished,' she said with heavy sarcasm when he closed the bathroom door, but he only glanced impassively at her and marched on to look in the kitchen. The nerve of the man! Sheona couldn't help but look in after him, and her heart sank. Petra had breakfasted late and hurriedly—too hurriedly to wash up or even clear the bran packet and dirty dishes from the table.

He had a swift look around and said with the tactlessness she was coming to expect of him, 'This place isn't exactly a palace, is it?'

'We're not much bothered by visiting royalty,' she snapped. 'If you'd waited for an invitation we'd have rolled out the red carpet.'

Marcus Drummond frowned at her. 'Who's the "we"?'

'Mind your own business!'

'I am. Your business is very much mine now, Miss Murray, and the sooner you realise it the better. I haven't been looking for a red carpet, either. I've been looking for a room where we can talk, if such a place exists in this ruin. You'd better lead on.'

'This "ruin" happens to be my home, and the only place you're going is straight back out of it!' she raged.

'Don't talk such rot.'

Sheona felt something very close to pure hate. She felt something else, too—inadequacy. She was tall, but he was taller still and twice as solid. He was right, curse him, she *had* talked rot. There was no way she could throw him out. She could always scream the neighbours in, but she hadn't the nerve to make that sort of fuss for anything less than rape—and, whatever Drummond wanted, it couldn't be her body. Shireen's, maybe, but definitely not hers. She didn't exude sensuality the way her sister did.

Somehow that wasn't very comforting, either.

Furious with him, just as furious with herself, she ground out, 'What a bastard you are.'

For the first time he smiled. Sheona's heart gave a funny sort of lurch but it soon straightened out when he agreed, 'Precisely, and I'm delighted you're more astute than your twin. I didn't expect us to establish such a good understanding quite so quickly. I'm sure we'll work very well together.'

Work together? What the devil did he mean? Baffled, she gaped at him. Drummond put a finger under her chin and closed her mouth. She recoiled from his touch, then wished she'd stood her ground and bitten his finger instead. Perhaps he saw the regret reflected in her eyes because he didn't give her a second chance.

He turned away and opened the last door on the ground floor, and this time he walked in, clearly expecting her to follow. Light from her sunny studio streamed along the passage, banishing its gloominess and highlighting its quaint old charm. It was a pity he hadn't started at this end, Sheona thought; then he might not have been so critical about the house.

Suddenly, though, she found herself wishing she'd been able to keep him out of her studio. Here she expressed the person she really was, and that made her feel more exposed and defenceless than if she'd been stark naked under his piercing gaze. It was her innermost self he was inspecting as his eyes roamed from the sketching she'd done that morning to the walls and shelves decorated with examples of her completed work.

Her brief but stormy experience of him convinced her he wouldn't be flattering. So unreasonable was her dread of his scorn that once more she felt he was dragging her back to that unhappy time when even imagined disapproval could make her physically sick. At least, Shireen had told her it was imagined. Deep down inside, she'd known better.

To protect herself she attacked before he did. 'Whatever your opinion, keep it to yourself,' she told him frostily. 'I'm not interested.'

Marcus Drummond gave her a cool, assessing look. 'This is your work, then?'

'Which you are interrupting.'

'Only because you interrupted mine.' He sat down on her adjustable chair, his long legs stretching out towards her as he scrutinised her blatantly from top to toe.

She couldn't give him the same treatment. With her glasses on he was too far for her to focus properly, but her simmering resentment was heating up to boiling-point. She didn't enjoy feeling like an ant under a micro-scope, nor did she like the way he was making himself at home, all uninvited!

She stood awkwardly where she was, declining to move a pile of sketches from the only other chair in the studio and relax herself. She'd hate him to get the idea he was welcome.

'Is Shireen pregnant?' He shot the question at her like another bullet that couldn't be ducked.

'No!' she exclaimed. 'At least, I shouldn't think so. She doesn't plan to have children while she's at the peak of her career.'

'Wise girl,' he approved. 'What about you?'

'My house-partner and I have enough hassle keeping up with the mortgage. We have a no-children pact until we sort ourselves out,' she replied frigidly. Not that this was any of his business, either, but she knew he wouldn't go away until he'd discovered whatever it was he'd come to find out.

'Where is he now, this house-partner?'

'She,' Sheona corrected. 'She makes pottery in the studio above this one, but at the moment she's at the shop where we sell our stuff. We take that in turns. We pooled our resources when we graduated from college to set ourselves up in business.'

She paused for breath, then ended tartly, 'In case there's anything else you'd like to know, I also have a scar on my knee where I fell on a nail as a child, a mole on my thigh and two fillings, both wisdoms.'

There was no shaming Drummond into stopping his impertinent questioning, though. He didn't even seem to know he was being impertinent. He leaned back in his chair and said, 'Make-up will fix the scar, the camera won't see the wisdoms but the mole might be a problem.

Take off that smock so I can see for myself what other problems you've got.'

Sheona was electrified. Her heart seemed to stop altogether, then pump furiously as she struggled to absorb the shock he had inflicted on her. He was talking as though she were the model, not Shireen, and as for letting his disapproving eyes dissect her further—never! Instinctively she clutched her smock around her, folding her arms across her bosom and hugging her waist.

'For heaven's sake, stop being so virginal,' he growled. 'I want to look, not touch.'

'B-but why?'

'I should have thought that was perfectly obvious. You, Sheona, are about to become Shireen for a few days.'

'No!' she gasped, horrified. 'No, no, no! I *hate* modelling.'

'I know you do,' he agreed smugly, 'so now you can stop sheltering Shireen and tell me where I can find her. OK, so we quarrelled, but it wasn't worth all this fuss.'

'I don't know where she is! I truly don't,' she cried in anguish, breaking into a cold sweat at the very thought of being thrust back before the cameras.

'You expect me to believe that?'

'It's the truth.'

Drummond looked at her long and hard, but he didn't say anything for a while. Sheona began to think he'd deliberately panicked her to trick Shireen's whereabouts from her. Now he'd found that he couldn't he would go away, leave her to her chosen, peaceful existence. She began to relax, then was promptly overwhelmed by panic again as he said at last, 'Then there's no choice. You'll have to stand in for Shireen until she turns up. That smock will have to come off. I need a good look at you.'

'No,' Sheona panted, backing towards the door. 'Never! You have no hold over me. You might think you're the best thing since sliced bread, but there's no way you can force me to do anything I don't want to do.'

She was halfway out of the door when he said with the silkiness she distrusted so intensely, 'I can ruin your sister.'

Sheona froze. Slowly, disbelievingly, she turned her head back to him. He was as relaxed as ever in her chair, and hate flickered like a live thing from her dark eyes as she challenged, 'You wouldn't!'

Drummond smiled. Confirmation was clear enough in that infuriatingly smug smile, but he reinforced the message with, 'You can bet your sweet life I'd ruin her before I let her ruin me. Or anyone else who gets in my way, for that matter. What do you think I am, a mouse that roars?'

Anything less mouse-like she couldn't imagine. Thanks to him, her beloved studio was no longer a happy place. The atmosphere was charged with tension, with the clashing of his ruthlessness with her loathing.

'You devil,' she breathed.

'That, too,' he admitted. 'You can hate me as much as you like but you will work for me—if you want to ensure that Shireen ever works again. Twins are supposed to be particularly close, aren't they? Very hot on the loyalty bit.'

He had her there and he knew it, curse him. She and Shireen might be totally different personalities but they were still inextricably linked. They didn't always understand each other, but they couldn't help but leap to each other's defence. Whatever the threat, whatever the cost. Growing up and apart hadn't altered that instinct one iota.

Sheona felt the resistance drain from her, leaving her limp and exhausted. He read defeat in the sag of her shoulders and, far from feeling compassion, he ordered, 'The smock, Sheona.'

She made one last effort to hold out against him. 'This contract—how am I supposed to know what it involves or whether she's even signed it?'

He drew a folded sheaf of papers from an inside pocket of his suit and held it out to her. She stretched to take it, not wanting to get one step closer to him than she had to.

As she read it Drummond summarised, 'It's signed and it's watertight. Shireen is contracted exclusively to my company for a fortnight, starting tomorrow, to make the follow-up commercials and poster shots to the ones we've already shot. We *cannot* change models midstream without wrecking the whole campaign and, as I've already told you, there are millions involved. No advertising agency, no manufacturer, will risk hiring her in future if it gets out that she's wilfully broken a contract of this magnitude.'

'And you'll make sure it does get out?' Sheona said bitterly.

'Get out? I'll sue her for every penny I can get. Everything's set up for filming. The male model, the film crew and equipment are hired, the location accommodation booked, and so on *ad infinitum*. That's too costly an operation in itself to cancel, and Shireen knows it. She's betting on her charisma and selling-power allowing her to take liberties, but she's betting on a loser. Nobody's that good, not even Shireen Murray. Advertising is a relentless and unforgiving business—and the law's the law. You can ruin your twin, or save her.'

Sheona had read and listened to all she needed to. She tossed the contract back to him as though just touching anything he'd touched tainted her. Then she took off her smock. She stood there, tall, shapely and seething with humiliation.

Her fingernails dug into the palms of her hands as his eyes roamed slowly over her. She wasn't wearing a bra and the fine wool of her sweater clung intimately to her full breasts and flat midriff. Her stretch jeans nipped in her already tiny waist and revealed the swelling curves of her thighs and every line of her long, shapely legs.

When he had looked long enough, Drummond said, 'Turn around.'

Sheona's nails bit deeper into her palms but she turned. Even in a bustling crowd of would-be models she had hated auditions, but this one-to-one intimacy was a thousand times worse. In the same situation, Shireen would have laughed and posed outrageously. But to Sheona it was utter degradation.

Finally he said, 'Couldn't be better. You're a dead ringer for Shireen.'

Sheona swung round and exclaimed, 'How did you know about me? Did Shireen tell you?'

'She talked about you, sure, but she didn't have to. There are pictures of the two of you as child and teenage models in her portfolio. Anyway, I've been in the business long enough to remember the ads you made together until you quit... what was it, five years ago?'

'Six,' she answered sulkily, 'and if you can remember that far back you should also know that your scheme has a fatal flaw. I might *look* like Shireen but that's as far as it goes. I simply don't have her charisma. I was once famed throughout the advertising business as the dud twin, the woodentop. Shireen "carried" me until I gave up. The best they could do with me was tuck me in the background.'

'Times change,' he replied dismissively.

'Not that much, they don't! I couldn't persuade a starving man to buy a loaf of bread, so I'll be instant death to whatever product you're pushing. I hate being

the centre of attention. I freeze up. And even you, Mr
Drummond, can't bluff or bully your way round that!'

'You underestimate me, Miss Murray,' he replied
calmly, then alarmed her by getting to his feet and
coming purposefully towards her. 'The glasses will have
to go,' he added, reaching out and lifting them off her
nose before she could stop him.

Suddenly he was sharply in focus. It was almost a
shock to see that the impression she'd gained of a
handsome man in a roughly hewn sort of way was absolutely spot on. No smooth Adonis, this, but a more
primitive, earthier type.

Sheona felt a quiver run through her, a gut reaction
that veered between excitement and alarm. Before she
could recover he grasped her shoulders and pulled her
against him, gazing deeply into her eyes as if seeking the
answer to a question he hadn't yet asked.

An involuntary gasp parted her lips at the contact of
her soft, supple body with his hard, unyielding one. She
was outraged—and something else as well, but he gave
her no time to discover what. Her pupils dilated as his
head came down to hers, and she watched him, mesmerised, until his lips covered hers. There was nothing
tentative about his kiss. It was a confident act of
possession.

She gasped again but the sound was lost as her breath
mingled with his. Her senses reeled as though her soul—
everything that made her Sheona Murray!—was mingling
with everything that made him Marcus Drummond.

Sheona tried frantically to retain control, but his kiss
was too forceful, too demanding. It was an intense
physical expression of the man himself…as she had come
to know and loathe him in such a tempestuously short
time.

No matter how hard she struggled she couldn't resist
him, couldn't deny the response unleashed from her in-

nermost being by the passionate power of his assault. She felt herself softening, surrendering, ceasing to care. Then she was released as abruptly as she had been grabbed. She was disorientated, shocked in a different kind of way.

'Not so frozen now, are you?' he asked harshly. 'With me around I think you can stop worrying about being the dud twin. You're made of everything Shireen's made of, and it isn't wood.'

Sheona's face burned as his words scorched and scarred her sensitive soul. He had contrived all that passion to prove a point, the brute! For a moment there, a brief but never-to-be-forgotten moment, she'd thought it had been irresistibly real, and that he had been surrendering, too...

She almost died of shame; then with all the power of her outraged, quivering body she raised her hand and struck him across the face. He must have seen the blow coming a mile away but he did nothing to evade it. He took its full force without flinching, and sounded completely unshaken as he told her, 'You owed me that. Now go and pack.'

'Pack?' she repeated disbelievingly.

He turned away from her, placed her glasses on the workbench and replied, 'Yes, pack. It's what suitcases are for.'

'Don't patronise me, Mr Drummond,' she snapped. 'What the hell am I supposed to pack for?'

'You can drop the "Mr Drummond". I think we know each other well enough by now to use first names. And you, Sheona, are packing to come with me.'

'I am not! Shireen's contract doesn't start until tomorrow, and I'll make my own arrangements to get to wherever I'm supposed to be.'

'You don't think I'm going to give you the chance to skip off to Shireen, do you? I'm not that naïve.'

'But I don't know where she is!' Such was her frustration, her outrage, that her voice almost broke.

'To skip off anywhere, if you're telling the truth,' he corrected.

'I won't. I promise I won't!'

'It doesn't make any odds. When I leave here you come with me. Whatever the true situation, I'm sure Shireen will return immediately she discovers I intend to use you in her place. Either to protect you—or to make sure there's no latent talent in you to challenge hers. Top models aren't the most secure of people. She thinks she has me over a barrel at the moment, and she's going to get a nasty shock when she discovers she's wrong.'

Sheona caught her lower lip between her white teeth and held on to it while she considered her options. If she had any. None materialised, so she said angrily, 'How is Shireen supposed to know I'm with you? We may be twins, but we're not telepathic.'

'You'll leave a note for your house-partner explaining that you've been called away hurriedly to fulfil a contract for Shireen, and won't be home for a few days. Shireen's bound to phone back to find out my reaction to her message, and your house-partner can tell her what's happened to you.'

Damn the man—he'd thought of everything! He was like some kind of evil Svengali. Was *he* the reason Shireen had run away? He'd talked about a quarrel, but somehow Sheona didn't think that was bothering her sister. Shireen had been too giggly, too excited, and anybody fleeing Marcus Drummond was more likely to be a frightened, nervous wreck. At least, Sheona knew that she herself would be.

'You're clever,' she admitted at last, 'but I'm afraid you've overlooked the obvious.'

'Which is?'

'That I wouldn't go anywhere with you. I wouldn't feel safe.'

'A simple demonstration that you're not as frozen as you think scarcely constitutes rape, and it's up to you whether the demonstration will be repeated or not,' he replied, sounding bored. 'As far as I'm concerned, if Shireen doesn't show up all your work for me will be before the cameras with plenty of chaperons, not alone on your back in my bed.'

'There's no need to be so crude!' she cried.

'Then stop behaving as if I'm going to drop my trousers and take you on the floor right now. I could have done that five minutes ago if I'd been interested.'

Hot blood rushed to Sheona's cheeks and she stuttered, 'How d-dare you?'

'Don't force me to show you just how much I'd dare,' he threatened. 'Go and pack—or I'll do it for you.'

The thought of him in her bedroom, his hands among her personal things, drained the colour from her face and she breathed, 'You wouldn't...'

'Try me,' he challenged.

CHAPTER THREE

THE tension between them was so intense that nothing less than a chainsaw could have cut through it. Sheona hovered on the brink of mutiny, her eyes riveted to Marcus's. She let him read the hate simmering in them, but he remained unmoved. She knew then that she was defeated, that there was no way she could wring any kind of concession out of him.

'When this is over don't call me, I'll call you,' she said with loathing.

'When this is over I'll have no reason to call you.' He picked up her glasses from the workbench. 'Don't forget these.'

Sheona snatched them from him and asked resentfully, 'What sort of things should I pack?'

'Something suitable for dining with me this evening, then formal and casual wear suitable for a temperature of over eighty degrees. We fly to the Seychelles tomorrow.'

'The Seychelles!' she gasped. 'What's wrong with a studio in London?'

'We're shooting the real thing. This is a big campaign. Too big for fake backgrounds. You do have a full passport, not just a European one?'

'Yes,' she answered bitterly, 'but you will live to wish I hadn't. I'm bound to muck up your precious campaign. You'd better pray as hard as me that Shireen shows up in time.'

'I think that appropriating you will guarantee that,' he replied smoothly.

'Appropriating!' she echoed contemptuously. 'Black-mailing is more like it.'

'Call it what you like, so long as you get moving.'

'How will we be travelling to London?'

'Car,' he replied as though she'd asked a really stupid question. 'I'll give you fifteen minutes to pack. After that you come with me whether you're ready or not. Where's your phone? I have some calls to make.'

'In the hall, and you can put the money to pay for your calls in the box beside the phone,' she replied wasp-ishly. 'Money's tight in this house.'

'Then you're in for a bonanza. From tomorrow you'll be getting Shireen's astronomical fee until she starts earning it herself. You'll be able to pay somebody to put the house right for you. Doesn't that make you feel better?'

'No, it doesn't! The house I can live with; modelling I can't. I found out a long time ago that there's more to life than money. It's a pity you didn't do the same.'

'Save the histrionics for the cameras,' he advised her coldly. 'They cut no ice with me.'

Sheona glowered at him in speechless rage, stalked out of the studio and up the stairs to her bedroom. He thought she was pretending to loathe modelling! Probably to save her face because she was no good at it. What did he know of the panic, the sick nausea that overcame her when everybody was losing their tempers with her because she couldn't 'act natural'?

Furiously she pulled down a set of cream leather suit-cases from the top of one of her wardrobes. She began to fling things into the largest case, beautiful things sent to her by her sister, who discarded clothes as frequently as she bought them. It was a standing joke between Sheona and Petra that if they ever went completely broke they could always open a second-hand dress shop.

But Sheona was far from laughing as she heaped underwear and nightwear on top of the clothes she had rapidly selected. Shoes, toiletries and other odds and ends she threw into a smaller suitcase, and snapped both lids shut.

She was left with little to put into the matching vanity case, which must have been packed to the brim before Shireen had tired of it. Cosmetics, though, were the tools of a model's trade, and Sheona had little use for them—although Shireen also kept her bountifully supplied with everything from lipsticks to body lotions.

Sheona made a modest choice of basic items, added her passport and glasses and closed the vanity case. She put the suitcases at the top of the stairs and returned to her bedroom to change out of her black sweater and jeans.

It was late afternoon and the warmth and light of the Indian-summer day was fading fast. Soon the chill of a true October dusk would strike, so she needed to wear something warm. On the other hand, Marcus Drummond's car was bound to be heated. For the first time Sheona dithered. What the hell, she thought, exasperated with herself. It was herself she had to please. She wasn't working for him yet.

As good as, a voice in her brain whispered, but she wouldn't listen to it. She didn't want Drummond to think she was intimidated enough to wear something suitable for the city, so she dressed comfortably in an orange and green tracksuit with a Bond Street label. At least it went with the orange chiffon tying back her hair, which she didn't have time to take down and put up again. She just brushed a few loose strands back and ran an orange lipstick swiftly over her lips.

There was no time to study the effect of the tracksuit, either. Naturally, it was one of her sister's hand-me-downs. Shireen liked vivid colours to set off her own dark colouring, although most likely the outfit had never seen the light of day outside of a London health centre. Sheona had never quite had the courage to wear it herself in Bournemouth, but then she'd never lost her fear of attracting attention to herself, either.

Drummond didn't matter, though. He didn't see her as a real, unrepeatable person—just as a convenient Shireen Murray clone. For Sheona, coping with his attitude was still like going back in time. It was only for a few days, though. She should be able to survive that, particularly if she could cling to the persistent feeling that none of this was really happening. With any luck, by the time it registered that it was real enough it would be over.

Sheona knew that her own attitude to the situation Drummond had thrust upon her was suspect, as crazy as clinging to a straw in a hurricane, but it was better than nothing. Muttering darkly to herself about men in general, and Drummond in particular, she grabbed the vanity case and left her bedroom.

Subconsciously she'd been listening to the murmur of his voice on the telephone, but as she ran down the stairs all was quiet and he was nowhere to be seen. She followed the rich smell of freshly percolated coffee to the kitchen, and found him calmly pouring himself a mugful. He glanced at her and lifted another mug down from a shelf next to the cooker. 'Black, white, sugar?' he asked laconically.

'White, no sugar. I thought we didn't have time for anything like that. You only gave me fifteen minutes!'

'Expecting you to be thirty,' he replied, pouring her coffee and handing it to her. 'That's how much time I could really allow.'

'Then why didn't you give me thirty?' she exclaimed, incensed as she thought of her frantic haste and the disorder she'd left in her normally neat bedroom.

'Because then I'd have expected you to take an hour, and we really don't have that much time. I have business to attend to before we dine,' he replied, unperturbed. 'Congratulations, Sheona, you've surprised me. You're unique among women. You actually know what time means.'

'You patronising——!' Sheona broke off as she fought the urge to fling her coffee at him. It was some moments before she regained some semblance of control, then she thumped the coffee down on the table.

Marcus, who'd accurately read every emotion mirrored on her lovely face, approved, 'I'm glad to see you're wise as well as unique. I can take the occasional slap, but I draw the line at a faceful of coffee. You and I nearly had a serious set-to there, and you're the one who'd have suffered for it.'

'Are you threatening me?' she stormed.

'Advising you, Sheona. We don't want to spoil our working relationship at this early stage, do we?'

Sheona was well aware his question was really a command. She seethed with pent-up emotions, and gritted her teeth as he continued, 'You can write the note to your friend while you're drinking your coffee.'

Another humiliating order, but for Shireen's sake she had to obey. Resentfully she pulled a notebook and pen from a dresser drawer, cleared a space at the table and sat down to write to Petra. How, in a few words, could she summarise all that had happened without alarming her friend? She chewed the end of the pen to no avail. Inspiration wouldn't come.

Marcus appeared to read her mind again because he dropped an engraved business card on the table and said, 'Leave my card with the note so that she knows everything is above-board. She can always contact my company if anything unforeseen happens.'

Unforeseen! Sheona silently raged. Everything about the man was unforeseen if only he had the sensitivity to realise it. But no, he persisted in regarding the most outrageous behaviour as ordinary... everyday! Not in her life, though. Not in Petra's, either.

She glared at his card and read, 'Drummond Advertising'. Below that on the left-hand side was a Mayfair address and telephone number. On the right-hand side was 'Marcus Drummond, Managing Director'.

She supposed she should be impressed but she wasn't in that sort of mood. Instead she said peevishly, 'Managing director, indeed! I feel sorry for your employees.'

'That should make a nice change from feeling sorry for yourself,' he replied, irritatingly unruffled. 'Meanwhile, the note, if you don't mind...'

Sheona minded very much, but she began to write, and she kept it simple. She told Petra only that she was doubling for Shireen for a few days while her sister was unavoidably delayed abroad. If there were any emergencies Petra was to contact Drummond Advertising and a message would be relayed to her. She suggested Petra hire a temporary assistant for the shop because she would be earning enough to cover any extra expenses.

Sheona tried not to grit her teeth as Drummond leaned across her shoulder to vet the note while she added her signature and attached his card. She didn't like being checked up on, nor did she like him this close to her. She could feel his breath on the nape of her neck and it made her feel... strange. Uneasy. Not the sort of uneasiness provoked by having to double for Shireen, but something different altogether.

She almost... almost... expected him to take another liberty and kiss her neck. Her nerves quivered expectantly, although she knew she was being ridiculous. She was doing as she was ordered, so she wasn't due for another 'demonstration'. She told herself crossly that she was sensing vibes that simply weren't there, except in her overwrought imagination.

The moments while he read the note seemed timeless, though, and to break the tension she asked sarcastically, 'Does it meet with your approval, Mr Drummond?'

'Marcus,' he corrected as he straightened up, 'and yes, it does. Brief, with no unnecessary details.'

Sheona smothered an indignant retort as she remembered what he dismissed as 'unnecessary details'—like his marching through the house as though he owned it, blackmailing her into doubling for Shireen, and kissing her with simulated passion to prove some odious point. At least, it had seemed to prove a point to him. As for herself, she was as unconvinced as ever.

'*Marcus,*' she said, stressing his name with even heavier sarcasm than she'd used so far, and standing up to face him, 'a good working relationship is an honest one, isn't it?'

'Yes.'

'Then you won't mind my saying that I honestly detest you!'

'Do you?' he asked, tracing her full lips with a surprisingly gentle finger. 'I wonder...?'

Sheona stepped back from him as though she'd been stung, and bit her lips to stop them from quivering at his touch. She snatched up her vanity case and told him stormily, 'My suitcases are ready at the top of the stairs but I won't—*I won't*!—go as far as the front door with you unless you keep your hands to yourself.'

'Then stop provoking me,' he answered pithily, and strode out of the room.

She provoking him! Sheona was too astounded to even gasp. The man was unbelievable. But she had to believe him and toe whatever line he cared to draw if she was to survive unscathed until her sister returned to save her.

Save her? It couldn't really be as bad as that, she tried to persuade herself as she left the kitchen and dawdled along the passage. She knew that it was, though. She also knew that she and Marcus were as incompatible as certain chemicals. Try to mix them and they exploded.

If she knew that why didn't he? He was the one who thought himself so all-fired clever! Her heart turned over as she saw he was already at the front door with her suitcases, impatience once more written across his rugged face. She had no choice but to join him, yet she had to force every step. She was full of fears, and one of them was the eerie feeling she wouldn't return to the house quite the same girl as she left it.

'Marcus...' She plucked at his sleeve with nervous fingers, quite forgetting she'd just had a fit at him for touching her.

'What?' He frowned down at her, his heavy eyebrows lowering and meeting forbiddingly across his nose.

Sheona stared up at him, searching his face anxiously for some sign of softening. She searched in vain. He looked tougher and more implacable than ever. Her courage failed and her fingers fell away from his sleeve. It was no use trying to appeal to his better nature. He didn't have one. 'Nothing,' she mumbled hopelessly, and walked past him.

She heard him slam the front door shut. It sounded forbidding, like his frowning face. The sound faded but it stirred up nervous echoes in Sheona's vivid imagination. Was that the sound, she wondered feverishly, that heralded the end of one existence and the beginning of another? She hoped not. In her overwrought state it sounded too much like doom...

Marcus, damn him, had no patience with the apprehension stamped so clearly on her face. 'Stop acting as though this is the last act of *Macbeth*,' he mocked her irritably. 'You're not going to end up a corpse—you're going on an unexpected holiday.'

'Is that what you call it?' she snapped back, his heartlessness reviving her flagging spirit like magic. 'You've dragged me away from my work, my home, my friends. You've——'

'I've brought a bit of excitement into your life,' he interrupted callously, leading her past her modest runabout and a row of other cars crammed bumper-to-bumper at the kerbside. 'For a few days you can *be* your sister instead of envying her, so stop making such a hypocritical fuss.'

'I don't envy Shireen!' she exploded.

'You're lying.'

'I'm not!'

'You're fooling yourself, then. That's worse.'

'You—you——' Sheona stuttered helplessly, her fury too great to be formed into words. Then she snapped her mouth shut. It was a waste of breath trying to argue with him. Once he made up his mind about something, that was it. 'I'm amazed somebody hasn't nominated you for God,' she grumbled, and was surprised when he laughed.

She looked at him a little shyly, unused to any human reaction from him, but he was stopping by a superb four-litre-engine saloon and unlocking the boot. A Jaguar, no less. Somehow, that wasn't a surprise. She couldn't think of a car more suited to the man, and the colour was right, too—red. For danger.

He put her suitcases in the boot and she added her vanity case. His eyebrows shot up. 'You don't mind being separated from your make-up for a couple of hours?' he asked, shutting the boot and unlocking the front passenger-door for her. 'For a beautiful woman, Sheona, you're definitely unique.'

Beautiful . . . he'd called her beautiful. Well, there was nothing startling about that, Sheona lectured herself as she ducked into the car and her artist's eyes automatically approved the leather parchment interior. She was a dead ringer for Shireen, so of course she was beautiful. The difference was that being beautiful had never meant anything to her until he'd said it.

All her life she'd wilted under the burden of looking like Shireen because the life that went with it hadn't suited her at all. Now, for the very first time, she was glad, and she didn't know why. Surely a compliment from a man she detested couldn't have wrought such a change? She was so unnerved that she had to reject the compliment, put Marcus firmly in his rightful place so that she could slip back into hers.

'I can't possibly be unique,' she told him as his powerful frame filled the space beside her, 'I'm an identical twin.'

'That's what I thought, but it goes no deeper than the skin, does it?' Marcus replied, switching on the engine and smoothly manoeuvring the Jag away from the kerb.

Sheona didn't answer. So he'd noticed, just as everybody who'd ever known her and Shireen had noticed, that she hadn't the vivacity, the inner sparkle, to back up the beauty they shared. In spite of his shameless embrace, his faked 'demonstration' passion, he thought precisely what everybody else thought—that she was the dud twin.

So what? It was a hurt she'd learned to live with. A hurt that had ceased to hurt, in fact, until he'd stirred it all up again. Her resentment towards him flared anew and she kept well away from the wide arm-rest separating their two seats. He was using it and no way was she going to risk touching him, however accidentally.

The silence that had fallen between them didn't appear to bother him. He seemed content just to drive, deep in thoughts of his own, threading the gleaming car effortlessly through the early Friday commuter rush to get away for the weekend.

Sheona stared out at the familiar grassed roundabouts and wide tree-lined roads that took them away from the city centre, away from everything that was known and familiar to her. Soon the scenery was unknown and Marcus's foot was pressing harder on the accelerator as they sped north-east to London. A hundred miles or so of being confined with a man who was so indifferent to her that he'd forgotten she was there.

Well, that suited her, didn't it? Imperceptibly, she began to relax. The comfortable bucket seat seemed contoured to her body, and the silky-smooth engine was quiet and restful. She leaned back and let the tension drain out of her. Idly she watched Marcus's hands on the steering-wheel. Such capable hands. She found herself remembering the strength of them when he'd grasped her shoulders, and a quiver ran through her. Hurriedly she turned her head away, seeking something less dangerous to watch.

'Cold, Sheona?'

So he hadn't forgotten about her. She almost quivered again but she managed to suppress it. 'No, I'm too warm, if anything.'

'Take off your top, then.'

'I can't. I haven't anything on underneath.'

'Now there's a thought,' Marcus murmured provocatively.

Sheona was startled. She'd been so convinced he regarded her as nothing but a model substitute for Shireen that it hadn't crossed her mind he might be attracted to her. But, no, that couldn't be right. He'd have been a darned sight nicer to her if he had. His remark must have been just one of those silly comments men seemed compelled to make to any woman who didn't look like the back of a bus.

Her silence seemed to amuse him. 'Relax,' he said. 'I'm good, but even I can't handle a Jag and a woman at the same time. I never mix work with pleasure, anyway. There are problems enough without making unnecessary waves.'

For some reason his reassurance aroused as much chagrin as relief in her, and she could only be grateful when he adjusted a control on the walnut-finished dashboard and cool air blew her way. 'That better?' he asked.

'Yes, thank you.'

'You're a polite little thing when you're not angry,' he observed.

Sheona thought he was mocking her and she replied huffily, 'If you can call all five feet nine inches of me little.'

'Oh, I know how tall you are. I also know you're twenty-two, you have a fine arts degree and you're building a reputation for yourself with hand-painted china. I know lots of other stuff about you, too. Shireen sings your praises regularly. She also has a plate on the wall in her flat with portraits of you both painted on it. A very fine piece of work.'

'Thank you,' she replied stiffly, sure he was patronising her again. She knew her work was good, otherwise she'd never be able to make a living out of it, but she couldn't believe or accept any praise from him. Somehow, in some obscure way, she felt she'd be caught out if she did.

'That piece was Shireen's idea,' she explained. 'She thought it might bring in commissions for me, and she was right. A one-off piece of hand-painted china makes a good Christmas or birthday present, specially for people who have everything else.'

'I'll remember that.'

Sheona didn't believe for a moment that he would, and fell silent again. Besides, she needed time to think. Marcus had said he never mixed business with pleasure but he seemed to know Shireen exceptionally well. More to the point, he knew her flat.

Her twin might be fun-loving and easygoing, but she was very choosy over whom she invited home. She was in the public eye so much that she needed her privacy and guarded it fiercely. 'The way to survive in this frenetic business,' she'd once told Sheona, 'is never to let the hassle of work get a foot over your own front doorstep.'

Yet Marcus had been over that doorstep...

'What did you and Shireen quarrel about?' she asked suddenly.

'That's strictly between Shireen and me.'

Sheona refused to be snubbed. 'Was it business or personal? She's my sister, you know.'

'I know. You wouldn't be here if she wasn't,' he replied irritably. 'Why don't you ask something more constructive? You haven't shown the slightest interest in the product this campaign is launching.'

'That's because I haven't any interest in it.'

'You will,' he promised, his harshness returning with a vengeance. 'If Shireen doesn't turn up sharply this product will become as much a part of your life as I am.'

'But you're not a part of my life!' she denied hotly.

Marcus just smiled.

Sheona hated the way he smiled. It was too cold, too calculating, with nothing in it at all that she could warm herself by... and suddenly she wanted very much to be warmed.

CHAPTER FOUR

THEY hadn't spoken to each other for ages. The silence wasn't particularly comfortable, but then, nothing about Marcus was. Sheona had slumped so deeply into a miserable reverie of all that had happened since he'd heavy-footed his way into her house and her life that it was some time before she noticed they were no longer heading for central London.

She stared in surprise at the quiet countrified lane they were cruising along and asked, 'Where are we?'

'Richmond upon Thames. It's only a few miles from my office in Mayfair but it's a different world.'

Sheona caught a glimpse of the Thames, flowing tranquilly between grassy willow-lined banks, and privately agreed that nothing could be further from the hassle of the city. 'It's lovely,' she said, 'but what are we doing here?'

'We're home.' He turned into a driveway that curved through massed bushes of late-flowering hydrangeas until the vista opened up to broad expanses of neatly clipped lawns. Snuggling peacefully in the middle of them was a sprawling two-storeyed house, the upper windows gabled by the graceful downward sweep of the roof.

Home, Sheona thought. It had such a reassuring sound, except that this was Marcus's home, and nothing about him was reassuring, either. Still, the house was old enough to look mellow and welcoming in its idyllic setting, and she gave credit where it was due. 'It's beautiful.'

'Thank you.'

He sounded vague, as though his mind was really on something else, and she was annoyed enough to comment, 'I suppose this house comes under the heading of "the fruits of success".'

'Don't knock the fruit before you've tasted it,' he answered in his abrupt way, driving past the front door and on to a quaint old coach-house that had been converted into a garage. The door opened automatically as he flashed a remote-control beam at it.

Sheona felt thoroughly crushed again. As soon as he'd driven in and parked she got out of the car before he could help her. Two could play the take-it-or-leave-it game, she thought crossly, and although she was a late starter there was no harm in being a good finisher.

Marcus got her cases out of the boot as she reached for her vanity case, then she was following him to a side-door of the main house. It opened before they reached it and a diminutive elderly lady stood there. She wore a long embroidered robe and she was wreathed in smiles.

That wasn't all she was wreathed in, either. Chains and necklaces jostled for space around her plump neck, bangles and bracelets jangled at her wrists, and Sheona could hear rather than see the bell anklets concealed by her gown. Rings flashed from her fingers and a red rose was tucked into the wide braids of white hair wound around her head.

'Cordelia,' Marcus said affectionately, and stooped to kiss her on the cheek. Sheona was startled. This was a gentle Marcus she hadn't seen before, could scarcely believe existed. As he straightened up he added, 'I hope I haven't caused you too much trouble.'

Never mind about the trouble you've caused me, Sheona thought, miffed, but Cordelia was laughing, 'When I can't cope with an unexpected guest it will be time to throttle me with my own beads.' Her startlingly blue eyes moved to Sheona, and she went on, 'So this is the other twin. Perhaps your crazy scheme will work, after all. She's Shireen to the life.'

So Shireen had been here, too. Sheona wondered again how much of her sister's relationship with Marcus was business and how much was personal. She also wondered who the sweet old lady was, then Marcus said, 'Cordelia, meet Sheona. Sheona, meet my favourite dragon.'

'A friendly dragon.' Cordelia chuckled at the bewilderment on Sheona's face. Then she looked at her more closely and continued sympathetically, 'You poor darling, you look dreadfully harassed. Were you happy to take your sister's place or has Marcus bullied you abominably?'

'He's bullied me abominably.' Sheona didn't bother to mince matters. Why should she? Marcus never did!

Cordelia didn't seem the least surprised. She tucked her plump arm through Sheona's and drew her into the house. 'He always was a naughty boy. Impossibly headstrong. You must teach him to mind you. He will if he likes you, you know.'

No, Sheona didn't know. Marcus had never shown the least sign of liking her. But naughty boy! Cordelia spoke with the indulgence of a mother, and yet that couldn't be. There wasn't the slightest physical resemblance between them.

But whoever Cordelia was—and how like Marcus not to explain!—Sheona felt immeasurably relieved that there was another woman in the house. Never, ever would she forget Marcus's belief that he could have taken her within minutes of meeting her—if he'd been interested. That remark still stung. Always would . . .

Sheona found herself drawn into a passage half-panelled with polished oak. Cordelia was either too old or too plump to hurry, or she didn't believe in living life at Marcus's pace, because he'd gone on ahead and vanished.

Sheona didn't feel grateful, she felt dumped.

Cordelia didn't appear to notice and she continued her previous remarks by asking gently, 'Do you like Marcus?'

'No, and he doesn't like me, either.'

'Ah,' Cordelia breathed as they began to climb a solid-oak staircase, 'then I don't think I will dine with you this evening. Bad vibes upset my digestion.'

Sheona was conscience-stricken. Whatever she had against Marcus, it was none of Cordelia's fault. 'You mustn't let me push you out!' she exclaimed. 'I'd feel awful. Besides, I'd be only too happy to eat in my room.'

Cordelia raised a pair of spectacles that were clipped to one of the chains around her neck, settled them on her little nose and looked hard into Sheona's anxious eyes. 'Appearances only,' she said at last.

'I beg your pardon?'

'I mean you're not really like your twin at all. If anybody tried to push Shireen out she'd push back. You're—softer.'

'Competition's fierce when you're a top model,' Sheona replied defensively as they reached the top of the staircase and began to walk along a red-carpeted passage. 'Shireen has to be pushy.'

'Of course,' Cordelia replied mildly, opening a door and inviting Sheona to enter with a gesture that set the bangles on her arm jangling.

Sheona found herself in a large bedroom decorated in subtle shades of yellow and brown with flower-sprigged curtains and matching cushions and bedspread. It was both luxurious and homely, and she said impulsively, 'What a lovely room. Lovely but welcoming.'

'The house has been in the Drummond family for generations and it shows,' Cordelia replied comfortably.

'Traditionally, the parents retired here and the eldest son stayed on Drummond Island to run the plantation. Marcus was an only son, though, and he's changed all that. He lives a dual life—here and on the island. It's hectic but he makes it work.'

Sheona was bewildered. 'Drummond Island?'

'It's in the Seychelles,' Cordelia enlightened her. 'That's where you're going tomorrow. Of course, tourists are more important now than the plantation, but there won't be any there during the filming. Marcus arranged all that ages ago. There are two monsoon seasons, but October is calm and not *unbearably* hot. That's why they're filming the next three commercials all at once, to get the right continuity and conditions.'

'Three commercials,' Sheona echoed, her heart sinking as the enormity of Shireen's failing to meet her contractual obligations struck home even harder. 'But the Seychelles are in the Indian Ocean! It must cost a fortune to film out there.'

'Marcus hasn't kidnapped you for nothing. He has a massive investment as well as the good name of his agency to protect.' Cordelia paused, then added delicately, 'It was kidnap, wasn't it?'

Sheona, irritated by Cordelia's calm acceptance of Marcus's high-handed ways, was unable to stop her bitterness from surfacing. 'No, it was blackmail,' she snapped. 'I have to co-operate with him or he'll make sure Shireen never works again!'

'Oh, dear! That sounds perfectly dreadful, but I expect you'll enjoy yourself once you get over the shock of it all. Marcus always knows what's best for everyone.'

Sheona was so taken aback that she found the nerve to demand, 'Who are you?'

'Didn't Marcus explain? Well, I did say he was a naughty boy.'

'Marcus isn't a naughty boy!' Sheona exclaimed, incensed. 'He's a full-grown, arrogant, overbearing brute—and I don't care if you *are* his mother. I'd say the same to anyone.'

'You say whatever makes you feel better,' Cordelia soothed, 'but actually I'm what Marcus calls his second mother. His real one died giving birth to his sister, Annabelle.'

'Oh, I'm sorry,' Sheona replied inadequately, feeling all kinds of a fool for allowing her temper to make her so tactless.

'It was all a long time ago. His mother was Delia Drummond, a very fine actress, and I was her dresser. I couldn't make the grade as an actress myself, you see, so I stuck as close to the stage as I could and just enjoyed being theatrical. I became a part of her success and her family, and sometimes I got walk-on parts. Those were *brilliant* years, and they lasted until Delia died so tragically.'

She paused and sighed. Sheona was trying frantically to think of something apt to murmur, something that wasn't impossibly trite, when Cordelia recovered and went on cheerfully, 'Never mind, the knack in life is to remember the good and forget the bad, isn't it? Anyway, I'd mostly raised Marcus myself as Delia was always so busy, so it seemed natural to take on the baby as well. Marcus was twelve at the time and as much of a handful as he is now, but his heart's in the right place.'

'Is it?' Sheona asked sceptically.

'Yes.' Cordelia sounded absolutely convinced about that.

Sheona was just as convinced that he didn't even have a heart, but she said nothing and allowed Cordelia to rattle on, 'Of course, Marcus has been leading his own life for years, and so is Annabelle now. She's twenty and has another year to go at university. I'm back on the stage—as an amateur, but it's still tremendous fun!'

Sheona, rapidly doing her sums, worked out that Marcus was thirty-two. She was surprised. He seemed so much older than that—not in looks, no, but in attitude, authority.

Before she could ask where his father fitted into the story, Cordelia said, 'There, now that you know Marcus's background I dare say all this will seem less strange and you'll start to enjoy yourself sooner. I hope so, anyway. I *do* like people to be happy. The bathroom's through that door over there and you have loads of time to relax before dinner. It will be delivered promptly at eight.'

'Delivered? Then I will be eating in my room,' Sheona replied, relieved.

'Certainly not,' Cordelia scolded. 'I meant dinner will be delivered to the house. I've ordered Chinese. I hope that's all right, but I'm going to drama rehearsals this evening, and I'm not much of a cook. Normally the housekeeper would cope but it's her day off and she didn't know a guest was expected. Neither did I until Marcus phoned this afternoon to explain what had happened. Naturally, I came straight over to the house to prepare for you.'

Sheona stared at her in dismay. 'Don't you live here?'

'Not any more. I prefer the flat above the old coachhouse. I may be old, but I have my own life to lead. So,' she added with a smile, 'does Marcus.'

'Me, too, not that he spares a thought for that!'

'My dear, why are you so bitter? What exactly has Marcus been doing to you?'

Sheona, given the perfect opportunity to relate all she'd suffered at his hands, suddenly found she didn't want to discuss him with anybody else. It was too personal, too *hurtful*. She shrugged her shoulders and replied evasively, 'It doesn't matter. I expect I'm still adjusting to having to double for Shireen. I hate modelling and it isn't like her to skip off. She's normally so professional.'

'We all step out of character sometimes,' Cordelia replied easily. 'Think how boring we'd be if we didn't.'

She smiled and went away, leaving Sheona staring at the door closing behind her and thinking, I never step out of character. Does that mean I'm boring?

That question did nothing for her self-confidence, but she noticed that, wherever Marcus had vanished to, he'd called in here first. Her suitcases were just inside the door. Dumped, like herself. That hurt, too. She didn't know why. She should be glad to be free of him for a while.

She wandered dispiritedly over to one of the dormer windows. Through the deepening dusk she could just discern acres of lawn sloping gently down to where ancient weeping willows trailed graceful leafy branches into the river. How peaceful it all looked. But Marcus owned all this magnificence, and anybody less peaceful she couldn't imagine...

Sheona glanced at her watch and then went to look at the bathroom. Yellow and brown, just like the bedroom, with fluffy fresh towels laid out, fresh bars of soap, fresh bath-oil, fresh everything. It was an invitation Sheona couldn't resist.

She unpacked a few things she would need overnight, then filled the tub and lay in the steaming fragrant water, trying to soak away the tensions of the day, tensions thrust upon her by her dictatorial host. A few short hours ago she hadn't even known him, and now her whole life was his to command.

Strangely enough, her resentment eased into a kind of acceptance of her fate and she felt almost relaxed as she shampooed and then blow-dried her long dark hair. Both

Marcus and Cordelia appeared to think she'd been given an unexpected holiday, as though she'd won some kind of prize. It wasn't what she thought herself but, since she had no choice, it made sense to go along with their attitude. If she could... and if Marcus didn't upset her again...

Sheona chose a high-necked long-sleeved tube dress to wear for dinner. It was simply designed in fine cream jersey, belted casually at the hips, and looked elegant without being too dressy. Shireen, no doubt, would have added dramatic earrings and pinned up her hair so that just a few tendrils curled sexily about her face.

Sheona, though, didn't want to look as if she'd taken pains with her appearance. She wore no jewellery at all, added no make-up to her vivid natural colouring, and let her glossy black hair fall freely down her back.

Marcus Drummond could make what he liked of that, she thought defiantly. And yet deep down she knew that she looked naturally stunning. Wanted to look stunning...

Whatever was happening to her?

She didn't want to delve into that and, perversely, having taken great care to be ready on time, she let eight o'clock come and go. Marcus was her host. It was time he remembered it.

At five-past eight, just as her nerve was beginning to fail, there was a staccato knocking at her door. She forced herself to open it leisurely, but still found her heart thumping as she gazed up at Marcus. He looked smoother, more conventionally handsome in a dinner suit, white shirt and dark tie, but nothing had changed about his expression. It was as disapproving as ever as he said, 'Unless you find cold Chinese food exciting, I suggest you come downstairs immediately.'

'Nobody told me where to find the dining-room, and I didn't fancy blundering around the house by myself,'

she answered, joining him in the passage and closing her
bedroom door behind her. 'I just had to hope you'd remember eventually that you had a guest. That's what a
host is supposed to do, isn't it?'

Marcus's frown vanished and he said appreciatively,
'Bitch.' His eyes roamed with lengthy deliberation all
over her and he corrected, 'Magnificent bitch. You look
absolutely stunning.'

It was what Sheona wanted to hear, and yet it made
her lose her composure. She said hurriedly, 'If you think
anything including the word "bitch" is a compliment,
I don't. To me, it's just offensive.'

'That's a pity. It suits you to be bitchy. Brightens you
up.'

So I *am* boring when I'm my normal self, she thought,
her flash of spirit deflating like a burst balloon. She
wished she could be less conscious of him as they walked
down the stairs together, but his shoulder was almost
touching hers, putting her unbearably on edge. She
hadn't yet learned how to cope with being this aware of
a man. It had never happened to her before.

'We'll have to skip the pre-dinner sherry,' Marcus said
as he led her through the square panelled hall and along
a blue-carpeted passage. 'No time.'

Sheona felt a pang of conscience. 'I hope Cordelia
isn't cross with me.'

'Cordelia is never cross with anyone. She has the gift
of happiness.'

'She must have if she can get along with you.'

Marcus was about to open a door but he stopped and
frowned down at her. 'Do you find me so very hard to
get along with?'

'Not hard,' she grumbled. 'Impossible.'

'I see.' His face was inscrutable as he ushered her into
the dining-room. Muted wall-lights shone a soft pink
glow on a large expanse of polished table. It was set

exquisitely with a bowl of pink roses, silver candlesticks, crystal glasses, gleaming cutlery and a rose-patterned dinner service.

Cordelia was transferring tureens from a serving trolley to the table. She looked up with a smile and whipped a cover from one of the tureens, releasing steam and the appetising aroma of chicken and mushroom soup. 'Do be seated, Sheona,' she invited, lighting the pink candles and shaking out the match as the wicks burned brightly.

Sheona, suddenly ravenous, sighed with an instinctive pleasure that parted her full lips into an appreciative smile. She didn't notice the softening of Marcus's face as he glanced quickly at her, his brown eyes intent under their dark brows. All Sheona knew was that all this was a world away from the evening meal she and Petra normally threw together—too busy or too hungry to take much trouble—then ate in the kitchen because the dining-room was still designated a disaster zone.

This was a different way of living altogether, a way she could so easily get used to. Except that Marcus went with it, of course.

She came to as he put a hand under her elbow, but for once she didn't object to his touch as he led her to a chair. It was at the side of the table, close to the chair at the top which she guessed was his. So only the top half of the table was being used, then. In other circumstances that would have been cosy.

Her eyes instinctively followed Marcus as he went to a sideboard and uncorked a bottle of wine. There was a compelling quality about him which he seemed entirely unaware of, and which she found impossible to resist. She was trying to figure out what it was when the faint click of the door shutting made her turn her head.

Cordelia had gone, leaving her alone with Marcus. She must have forgotten something, Sheona thought. Then she noticed the table was only set for two. She felt a jolt of alarm out of all proportion to the occasion, and half rose. 'Isn't Cordelia . . . ?' she began, and felt Marcus's hand on her shoulder, firmly pressing her back into her chair.

'Cordelia would rather be on time for her rehearsal than dine with us,' he said, keeping his hand on her shoulder until he felt the resistance go out of her. 'I didn't think you'd object. After all, Shireen's flitting off has upset her day almost as much as yours and mine.'

'She told me bad vibes upset her digestion,' Sheona argued.

'She was looking for an excuse to get away. She's always been besotted by the stage.'

'Are you sure? I offered to eat in my room. I'd much rather do that, anyway.'

'Honestly?' Marcus put a hand under her chin and forced her to look up at him, his eyes demanding the truth from her.

Sheona endured the intensity of his gaze for as long as she could, then her eyes slid away to the beautifully set table, the wine sparkling in the glasses, the food waiting to be eaten, and the necessary lie wouldn't come. 'No, not quite honestly,' she was forced to admit, 'but almost.'

Marcus relaxed and smiled. Sheona wished he wouldn't do that—smile and look so nice when she was least expecting it. It made her relax, too, and she'd really rather not—not while she was alone with him and never knew from one moment to the next when he would turn surly again.

'You're truthful, Sheona. I like that about you. There are other things I like as well. Do you think you could risk trying to like me, too?'

She felt a funny little flutter in her heart and faltered, 'Why?'

'Why not?' he replied as he ladled soup into her bowl.

Sheona watched the rose pattern disappear under the creamy soup, and played nervously with her spoon. 'Cordelia's been talking to you, hasn't she? Because I grumbled about you. Well, there's no need to be nice to me on her account. I hate hypocrisy.'

'I'm suggesting we become friends, not lovers. I don't see what's hypocritical about that.'

'That's because you haven't been bullied and black-mailed into being here!' she exclaimed indignantly. 'Friends are people I trust, and I could never trust you.'

Marcus placed his hand over hers. 'I've been hard on you, but I can be different. I could teach you to trust me, if you'd let me.'

His touch was too light to be threatening. In fact, it was strangely comforting, so much so that she snatched her hand away. It was a panic reaction to feeling suddenly vulnerable. She regretted the snub immediately, but it was too late.

Marcus withdrew his hand and made no further attempt to touch or befriend her. Sheona felt a searing sense of loss. For what, she didn't know...

CHAPTER FIVE

MARCUS talked politely and impersonally during the soup, the perfect host. It was as though he'd deliberately put their stormy relationship into neutral by sticking to non-controversial subjects like books, films and the theatre. Sheona, glad of a respite, gratefully followed his lead. It was all very unreal, considering the situation they were in, but it was a lot less hassle.

For the main course she chose sweet and sour prawn balls, fried rice, beansprouts, bamboo shoots and water chestnuts, and she commented as Marcus helped himself to beef chow mein, 'Cordelia seems to have ordered every dish on the menu. She's quite a character, isn't she?'

'She's a genuine character, not a pseud. The peace, love and happiness of the flower-power era suited her down to the ground. She's stuck to it and doesn't give a damn what anybody thinks.'

'I've noticed.' Cordelia seemed to be a safe subject, and Sheona wondered what else she could say about her. Inspiration struck and she went on, 'She was telling me you have a sister.'

'You won't be meeting Annabelle. She's back at Oxford for the winter term. She's reading literature.'

'Does she intend to be a writer?'

'Yes.'

Sheona never having met Annabelle, there didn't seem much more she could say about her, so she again risked a question that had been burning in her brain. 'Why *did* you and Shireen quarrel?'

58

Marcus shot her a quick look from under his heavy brows. 'Over my sister. Annabelle fancied herself in love with somebody very unsuitable. It would have run its course fast enough if Shireen hadn't interfered, but she couldn't resist stealing him away. I'm pretty certain she's with him now. What I don't know is where.'

'Oh!' Sheona was too startled to say anything else. Shireen might be a walking man-trap but she didn't poach. She didn't have to. Men chased her, not the other way round.

'Oh, indeed!' Marcus mimicked her so harshly that Sheona knew she'd blown the neutrality they'd been at such pains to preserve, and she hadn't meant to do that.

'I'm sorry,' she said inadequately.

'Not half as sorry as I am. Now my sister imagines her heart is broken, my model is off on a massive ego trip, and you can't do anything but ask stupid questions.'

'They are not stupid questions!' Sheona exclaimed indignantly. 'Shireen's my sister. She's the reason I'm here. I have as much right to know what's going on as you do!'

'Great. You can have a good old heart-to-heart with her when you meet up again, but leave me out of it. I only want to know Shireen professionally. Personally, I'd like to wring her neck.'

'Before or after mine?' Sheona snapped.

'Don't tempt me,' Marcus breathed, his eyes glowing threateningly.

Sheona was too angry to be intimidated, and she scoffed, 'No wonder Cordelia was so anxious to get off to rehearsals. She must have known what was coming.'

'Damn!' The rage went out of Marcus's eyes and he looked genuinely contrite. 'I promised her I'd be nice to you.'

'I wouldn't have appreciated the hypocrisy, any more than I appreciate your remarks about my sister,' she re-

torted, her anger fuelled by the realisation that his offer
of friendship, which she'd spent half the meal regretting
turning down, had only been made to please Cordelia.
'Shireen isn't spiteful and she doesn't need ego trips.
She wouldn't deliberately hurt Annabelle or anybody
else. She simply isn't like that.'

'I saw her vamping Mike Judson with my own eyes.
She couldn't have been more blatant about it if she'd
tried. I thought she was just amusing herself but, after
you phoned, I checked up on him. He's supposed to be
in London recording a new album but he's vanished,
too. It doesn't take a mathematician to put that particular two and two together. If only she'd left Judson
alone Annabelle would have been bored with him by
now.'

'Mike Judson the pop star?' Sheona exclaimed.
'What's so unsuitable about him? He's a multi-
millionaire.'

'He's not good enough for my sister. He's a
womaniser.'

'Oh, grow up! The man's not yet been born who's
good enough for somebody's sister, and all men are
womanisers before they settle down!'

Marcus's lips curled derisively. 'Now you not only look
like your sister, you sound like her.'

'Thank you. That's the nicest compliment that's been
paid to me for a long time.'

They glowered at each other, and then the telephone
rang. Marcus flung his napkin on the table and strode
across the room to answer it. The intervention hadn't
come a moment too soon for Sheona. She didn't have
the temperament to thrive on conflict, and such had been
the ferocity of their quarrel that she was actually shaking.
She clutched her hands together in her lap, desperate to
conceal her weakness from him, certain he would tramp
all over her if he suspected how sensitive she really was.

She listened to him uttering a series of terse 'yes's and 'no's into the telephone, hoping the respite would last. Unfortunately the call ended quickly. The person at the other end of the line must have realised that this was a bad time to make contact. Marcus had made it obvious enough.

He came back to the table and sat down again. 'I'm sorry about that,' he growled.

Sorry about what—the quarrel, or being interrupted by the phone? Sheona hadn't a clue, but she didn't want to stir things up again by asking. She forced her hands to pick up her own knife and fork, then concentrated hard to stop the cutlery clattering against her plate. She tried to eat but her enjoyment of the food had gone.

After a while Marcus asked abruptly, 'Have I upset you?'

'No,' she lied, suspicious of his sudden concern.

'Then stop pushing your food about your plate and eat it.'

Trust him to be observant when she least wanted him to be! Sheona put down her knife and fork. 'I've had enough, thank you.'

'No dessert?'

She shook her head. 'Just coffee, please.'

'I'll make some.' He stood up and began to stack the dishes on to the trolley Cordelia had left. Sheona, glad for something to do, helped him. It seemed strange to be doing anything as domestic as this with Marcus. Somehow, she'd thought he'd just walk away from the table and leave everything for the housekeeper to sort out in the morning. She simply hadn't had him down as a man to show any consideration for his staff.

She'd judged him, of course, on the lack of consideration he'd shown her, and she couldn't help wondering what made her so different. It might be because she was a constant reminder of Shireen, and he didn't like

Shireen. Then, like a bolt from the blue, it came to her that perhaps he liked Shireen too much—and had been as upset as his sister when she'd got involved with Mike Judson!

Sheona, stealing a glance at Marcus, thought losing would come hard to him. He looked like a man too used to winning to accept defeat readily.

But Marcus in love with Shireen! She didn't want to think about that. She really didn't. Somehow, it hurt.

The table was cleared. Marcus blew out the candles, and for some reason Sheona shivered. It seemed like the end of something, and yet the meal together hadn't been exactly successful. Nothing had improved in their relationship. If possible, it had deteriorated. Yet she still felt sad as the brown smoke from the gutted candles swayed and spiralled into oblivion.

'I wish...' she began impulsively, the words torn out of her.

'You wish what?' Marcus asked.

She thought she heard impatience in his voice, and it killed stone-dead the spontaneous emotion that had overcome her. 'Nothing,' she replied flatly, and yet she had really been wishing for so much—that they had found a way to overcome the antipathy between them...a way to being friends.

'It can't be nothing. Tell me,' he demanded.

'No.' Her voice was soft, final, sad. To snap herself out of her sudden and unreasonable melancholy she pushed the trolley towards the door and asked, 'Which way to the kitchen?'

'I'll do that.' He removed her hands roughly from the trolley and began to push it himself, adding irritably, 'I've never known a female make me as mad as you do. Whenever we're on the verge of something you just switch off.'

'The only thing you and I are ever on the verge of is a quarrel, and I hate quarrelling,' she replied, the strange sadness still with her. 'I haven't the temperament for it.'

'You could have fooled me.'

Sheona felt a surge of emotion suspiciously like hate at his insensitivity. She thought then that when she fell in love it would be with a man who was the complete opposite of Marcus Drummond. A man who would understand what she thought and felt without being told, and who wouldn't dream of bossing, bullying or browbeating her. If such a man existed the only thing he would have in common with Marcus would be this strange ability to make her feel one hundred per cent woman, one hundred per cent alive.

Involuntarily she sighed.

'What are you sighing for?' Marcus asked, shooting her another of his intimidating looks.

'The moon. I sigh for it regularly,' she replied, half honestly, half flippantly.

'And what does the moon represent for you?' he demanded, pushing the trolley into the large modern kitchen and over to the dishwasher.

'Everything you're not.' She hadn't meant to be that honest and, afraid she'd revealed more of her thoughts than she'd intended to, she hastily changed the subject. 'Shall I load the dishwasher while you make coffee?'

'Suits me.' He plugged in the percolator then leaned against a kitchen counter, surveying her moodily. She wished he wouldn't do that. It made her painfully aware of her every movement. She flinched inwardly as she clumsily clattered two plates together. She hadn't been this self-conscious since she'd abandoned modelling at the ripe old age of sixteen. Then it had been the cameras that had intimidated her—never a man on his own. But then, she'd never before met a man anything like Marcus.

'Do you have a boyfriend you want to contact?' he asked suddenly.

'No.'

'A girl who looks as you do?' he asked incredulously.

Sheona straightened up and glared at him. 'How do I look? Easy?'

Marcus glared right back, and snapped, 'Quite the reverse, and I'm damned if I know why you're so touchy. Just a hint of a compliment and you're spitting fire.'

The truth of what he said struck home so hard that Sheona felt guilty. This time he was in the right, no two ways about it. At times she was touchy—almost as unreasonable as he was. 'I'm sorry,' she apologised awkwardly. 'It's a hang-up from my modelling days. You know what photographers are like. They pay all these extravagant compliments to hype up a model and turn her on while they're clicking away, but it never worked for me. I knew the photographers would much rather be working with Shireen because she can turn it on like a tap, making it all so easy. Me, I was always hard work, and the more "stunning", "fantastic", "beautiful" and "terrific"s I heard, the more false they sounded, and the more wooden I became. That's why I've ended up so suspicious of compliments.'

'You've ended up with a head that needs unscrewing and putting back on properly,' Marcus replied pithily. 'This envy of Shireen is warping your life.'

Sheona's eyes flashed and she stamped her foot. 'I do *not* envy Shireen!' she exclaimed angrily. 'I just deeply resent everybody expecting me to be like her simply because I look like her. I should have known better than to try to explain. Nobody ever understands. Why should you be any different?'

It hurt, though, that he wasn't any different. It hurt so much that she slammed the dishwasher door shut, and raged on, 'I'll skip coffee, thanks. I prefer my own company and an early night! It beats anything else on offer around here.'

As she stalked past him he clasped his hands and applauded cynically, 'Bravo! A magnificent performance! Shireen couldn't have done better.'

Sheona gasped in outrage and swung a stinging slap at his satanically mocking face. This time she caught him by surprise, and the sound of the slap connecting with his cheek filled the room. It echoed in her ears as she stalked on until it was deafened by the kitchen door slamming behind her.

Just for once, raw and violent emotion didn't make her feel shattered or tearful. It buoyed her up, then boiled over again as she reached and slammed her bedroom door. She paced her room, back and forth, back and forth, looking for some other release for her rage. Finding nothing, she flung off her clothes and jumped into the shower, turning the automatic-mixer tap on full blast.

She had never, ever in her entire life been quite so heatedly and helplessly angry. She wanted to murder Marcus, she really did. She'd risked exposing a hidden facet of herself in an attempt to gain his understanding, but he hadn't understood. Hadn't wanted to! Oh, no, not him! He was Mr Clever-Clogs Drummond. He already knew it all.

Well, he knew nothing! Nothing about her, anyway. How *dared* he think she was acting? She would never forgive him for mocking and deriding her. Never!

Most of all she would never forgive him for not instinctively understanding the sort of person she was. For some peculiar reason she felt she should never have had to explain herself to him in the first place, that he should have known she was genuine. How, she wasn't sure. But he should have known!

Slowly, as the water continued to gush over her, her rage began to leave her. It wasn't exactly draining down the plug-hole with the water, but it had been too violent to be sustained for long. She was still angry, but she felt less murderous, less like slamming about.

She was also beginning to feel like a drowned rat. The cleansing water was no longer a benediction, it was an ordeal. She switched off the tap. Silence, but for the last gurgle of water down the drain. Which, come to think of it, was exactly where her relationship with Marcus Drummond was. And that's where it could stay.

'I hate him,' she muttered aloud between clenched teeth. 'He's a cynical, arrogant, overbearing brute. Sometimes, just sometimes, he acts almost...almost nice, and that's when he catches me out. But not any more!'

While she was muttering to herself she was drying herself just as fiercely. Her skin glowed by the time she'd finished and she padded, naked, into the bedroom, vigorously towelling her hair. She put on a pink Laura Ashley nightgown that had a demure bib top then fell in folds from her bosom to her feet. She couldn't be bothered to blow-dry her hair so she tied it up in a haphazard pony-tail, then sat cross-legged in the middle of her bed.

She'd meant to assume the lotus position to try to relax her tense muscles with some peaceful contemplation, but she couldn't concentrate. She was too edgy, too fidgety, too frustrated. Perhaps she shouldn't have flung away from Marcus like that. Perhaps she should have stayed for a slanging match after she'd belted him. She still felt as though she was in the middle of something, as though it wasn't over.

Just as she thought that, the door opened and Marcus walked in carrying a tray. 'Are you supposed to be looking sixteen or sexy or both?' he asked, his dark eyes taking in everything from her damp head to her bare toes.

'Get out!' she screamed, scrambling to the top of the bed, diving under the quilt and pulling it up to her chin. 'How dare you come in here without knocking? How dare you come in here at all?'

'If I'd knocked you'd have jammed a chair under the door-handle to keep me out,' he replied, 'and we have things to talk about. It's strictly business, so you can come out from under that quilt. Strange as it might seem to you, I'm not in the habit of raping my guests.'

'I need more than your word for that!' she retorted, too incensed to think what she was saying.

'My word is all you're going to get, my girl, so make the most of it. If you want to cower in that bed, you can, but frankly I prefer you on your feet and fighting. You show some spirit then, and I always admire spirit.'

'I don't want you to admire me!' Sheona exclaimed desperately.

Marcus slammed down the tray on a table and came towards her, tall and more powerfully threatening with each stride he took. His dark eyes narrowed to slits as he leaned down and grasped her shoulders, half lifting her out of the bed until their faces were just inches apart. 'Are you sure about that?' he grated harshly. 'I'm not. Shall we put it to the test?'

'No,' she gasped, trying to shrink away from him, but his hands were too strong, bruising her soft flesh. In the few short hours she'd known him, she'd already learned what it was like to be helpless in his arms. It mustn't happen again. It mustn't...

'No,' she repeated, this time her voice broken and begging. 'Please, Marcus, no!'

'Oh, for heaven's sake!' Marcus flung her away from him in disgust. 'You must have known I'd come up here to see you. What the hell were you sitting on the bed in

your nightie for if you didn't want to turn me on? Was
I supposed to believe that mad scramble for cover was
genuine? With all that flashing of legs and provocative
backward glances? Give me a break, will you? I wasn't
born yesterday.'

Sheona lay on the pillows where she'd fallen, staring
up at him in disbelief. She stuttered naïvely, 'W-why
should I want to turn you on?'

'You tell me. You're the tease.' Marcus was back at
the tray, pouring the coffee. His breathing was ragged
but his hands were steady.

Which was more than Sheona's were. She was shaking
like a leaf all over. She was also too stunned by the incredible things he was saying to even think of crawling
back under the doubtful safety of the quilt.

Marcus shot a moody glance at her shocked face and
thumped down the coffee-pot. 'If you don't want to back
up your act don't play your big scenes in a bedroom.
Not with me, anyway. I'm just not—tame enough.'

'I'm not acting! Can't you get that through your head?
Why should I?'

'Perhaps because you've finally got your big chance
to push Shireen's nose out of joint for a change, and
you're making the most of it.'

'That's an awful thing to say!'

'Is it? You'd be made and she'd be finished if I kept
you in the commercials. Isn't that what you're after?'

'No! How can you think such dreadful things about
me?'

'The only alternative is to accept that you're as innocent and genuine as you like to make out, and I find
that hard to believe of Shireen's twin.'

'Marcus...' Sheona stretched out her hands to him
in unwitting appeal '...you've got us both wrong. Shireen
wouldn't deliberately break up anybody's love-affair.
She's simply not like that.'

'I believe what I see with my own eyes. What do you believe in—Santa Claus? Why do you think she's skipped off, if not to play around with Judson?'

'I don't know,' Sheona replied despairingly. He'd ignored the appeal of her outstretched hands and she had to let them fall uselessly back into her lap.

Marcus studied her for a long moment, then asked in his abrupt way, 'Milk, sugar, cream?'

'Just cream, please,' she replied automatically, and took the cup just as automatically when he handed it to her.

He stood looking at her, his expression hard to read, then he reached down and pulled the quilt up over her again. Sheona flushed at her forgetfulness, looking thoroughly awkward and embarrassed as she stammered, 'I wasn't trying to—to——'

'Come on strong to me again? I know.' He spoke much more softly, much more reasonably, then turned from her to go back to the coffee-tray.

Her heart fluttered uncomfortably in her chest, not because she felt in danger again but because she felt almost . . . safe. Had she, against all the odds, managed to get through to him, touch some latent streak of compassion within him if nothing else? It seemed like it, and yet she felt desperately shy as he came back and sat on the edge of her bed.

Softly, afraid of starting another riot and yet determined to straighten things out while she had the chance, she asked, 'Does that mean you believe now that I'm not playing up to—to get your attention?'

'I'm thinking about it. Convince me.'

Sheona swallowed, then marshalled her arguments. 'You know I only came here to stop you ruining Shireen. You stressed yourself the loyalty that exists between twins.'

'That was the way I put it, but that's not necessarily why you came. You can't have liked always being out-shone by her.'

'Marcus——' Sheona's hands plucked nervously at the quilt as she sought for the right words to clear up his suspicions '—I've never resented Shireen's success, never wanted any part of it. All I resented was being the "other twin" because I was doing something I had no talent for. I only ever wanted to be an artist, and now that I am I'm happy. Really happy. Taking over from Shireen isn't a dream for me, it's a nightmare.'

There was deep silence when she finished, then Marcus put one of his big hands over her restless ones and stilled them. 'I've given you a rough time, then, haven't I?'

She looked up at him, feeling shyer than ever. 'Yes,' she whispered. 'I wish you'd tell me why.'

'Suspicion goes with the job,' he replied, his strong jaw hardening in a grimace. 'You'd be amazed what plots a beautiful woman can hatch up to remove a rival. I wouldn't have blamed you for trying to oust Shireen, but I wanted to be damn sure you knew you weren't fooling me. I won't be a pawn in somebody else's game.'

'That's what you've made of me,' she pointed out. 'I'm just a pawn between you and Shireen.'

'It won't be for long,' he replied, not attempting to deny it, 'and I'll try to make it easier for you in future. Let's drink our coffee, shall we? We've waited long enough for it.' He smiled at her, a real smile that held no cynicism or mockery.

Sheona found herself smiling back. She couldn't help it because a comforting warmth was creeping over her. The warmth of friendship? She hoped so. Marcus as an enemy was pure hell. Marcus as a friend was—nice. Something still troubled her, though, and she asked, 'You seemed to believe I was genuine enough when we first met. What made you change?'

Marcus gave her one of his long, hard looks, as though he was about to say something she sensed would be very important, then he changed his mind. He put his cup back on his saucer with a decisive click, a click that seemed to signal the end of their brief interlude of understanding. He began to rise, saying briskly, 'I don't want to keep you up all night. We make an early start tomorrow. I'll just give you a quick brief about the product and the advertising so far, then we'll call it a day.'

'Marcus.' Sheona reached impulsively for his arm, delaying him. How hard his muscles felt under her soft hand, how tough his skin compared to hers. She registered these strangely pleasant sensations before she continued, 'Please tell me.'

He paused and looked directly into her appealing eyes, then he said reluctantly, as though there were some things he preferred to keep to himself, 'When we first met you were wearing glasses. You haven't worn them since. When girls leave off their glasses it's usually because they want to look more glamorous. Why, if you hate modelling as much as you say you do, would you want to look more glamorous—unless to rival Shireen?'

'Is that all?' Sheona felt almost limp with relief, and then she giggled, 'Oh, Marcus, my glasses are only for very close, highly detailed work. I simply forgot I had them on when I answered the door to you.'

'Then why did you keep them on?'

'Self-defence. You were so aggressive that I preferred you fuzzy to properly focused. All right, so that was crazy, but I found you hard enough to cope with without actually seeing what kind of a devil I had rampaging through my house.'

'Devil?' he repeated with an arrested expression on his face. 'Is that the way I seem to you?'

'I wouldn't exactly call you a candidate for an angel, would you?' she teased, a mischievous smile lifting her lips entrancingly.

Then the smile froze on her lips. Suddenly she knew that he was going to kiss her. The intent was there for her to read in the darkening of his eyes, feel in the tenseness of his body.

And, just as suddenly, she knew that she wanted him to...

CHAPTER SIX

SHEONA had read about time standing still but she'd never experienced the sensation. She did now. Only Marcus's lips had any reality for her. She watched them hypnotically, unable to move as they closed on hers. She even seemed to stop breathing. She was in a total state of limbo, and dreamily she waited for him to bring her to life again. No longer was he a moody and unpredictable stranger. He was her partner, her future, her lover...

She felt his breath on her face and her eyes closed in anticipation. She didn't even wonder what was going through his mind, so sure was she that in this timeless moment they were truly together... in the purest sense of the word.

Then something happened. She didn't know what it was, but he pulled back from her, shrugging her hand from his arm, renouncing all contact, as though the momentary oblivion had been her phenomenon, not his. He got up from the bed and said with a roughness she didn't understand, nor felt she deserved, 'No, I'm not the stuff angels are made of. Remember that in future, and you won't get hurt.'

Hurt? She was already hurt! She felt the pain of misunderstanding, rejection, as she plunged into a different kind of limbo. Vaguely she was aware she must have completely misread the situation, made a fool of herself again. Now, more than ever, Marcus must be thinking she was his to take.

If he was interested, which he wasn't.

She was more than embarrassed: she was devastated. That hadn't been why she'd been so willing, so receptive—it truly hadn't! Those timeless moments hadn't been merely physical to her. They'd been almost... sublime. Or would have been if he'd shared them.

And yet she could have sworn that he had!

Now, in her devastation, she had to face that she'd been wrong about him again. He was too complex, too changeable, for her to comprehend. Every time the emotion of the moment tempted her to destroy the barrier between them she was the one who was destroyed. Marcus and the barrier remained intact.

Then why did he lead her on? Because sometimes... just now and again, and only momentarily... he imagined she was Shireen?

Sheona had sworn to him she'd never envied her twin, and it had been true. Now, though, she felt a stirring of envy, and she hated herself for it. She and Shireen might have gone their separate ways, but never before had anybody succeeded in driving any kind of wedge between them.

Until Marcus. He was more dangerous than even she'd supposed.

She watched him with broodily resentful eyes as he went back to the tray, and for the first time she registered that there was more than coffee on it. He picked up a decanter and waved it at her. 'Brandy?'

'No,' she replied shortly, 'and I'd rather you didn't drink in my bedroom, either.'

'I'll remember that in future. At the moment, however, I need a drink.'

Because I'm not Shireen? she wondered, her resentment hardening into animosity as he poured out a liberal measure. She watched him swirl the brandy around the glass, and drink it down in one go. My goodness, he wasn't going to get drunk, was he? Marcus sober was more than she could handle.

To her relief, he put the glass back on the tray and went over to the TV-video cabinet in one corner of the room. 'I'm going to show you the first commercial for the new product,' he said, completely businesslike again as he rearranged wires to set up the video. 'It's due to be screened next week at specially selected times when there's a large female audience.'

'Female?' Sheona asked interrogatively. Beautiful women were used to sell everything from cars to after-shave, so this was the first hint she'd had that the product was aimed at women.

'I knew you'd get interested eventually,' Marcus replied ironically, slotting a cassette into the video and glancing over his shoulder at her. 'It's a perfume.'

'Another one?' she mocked, not wanting to be interested, not wanting any sort of involvement at all. 'Has it got one of the provocative names that's all the rage at the moment to make it "different"?'

'You bet. It's called Slave.'

'You've got to be kidding!' Sheona exclaimed, sitting up straighter in the bed. 'This century has been one long struggle by women to get out of slavery—or haven't you heard about women's lib? None of us would dream of wearing a perfume with a name like that! I'm surprised Shireen's promoting it. She's a free spirit if ever there was one.'

'There's a twist,' Marcus replied coolly, picking up a remote-control beamer and coming back to the bed. 'Our commercials carry the message that using this perfume will make a slave of the man in a woman's life.'

I could use some of that, Sheona thought bitterly, but all she said was, 'Oh, that's definitely different.'

'Which is the name of the game,' Marcus replied, smiling.

Again, she wished he wouldn't smile like that. Especially as he sat beside her and leaned back against the bedhead as though she were no more of a distraction than the pillows he was crushing.

'Who dreamed up this campaign?' she asked in an effort to appear as unconcerned at his closeness as he was at hers.

'I did.'

'You?' That surprised her, and to conceal her very real interest she asked flippantly, 'I thought a boss-man like you hired people to do that sort of thing.'

'I do, but I have a special interest this time. My mother actually launched this perfume twenty-five years ago under the name of Love, but I won't bore you with the details.'

Sheona turned instinctively towards him and touched his arm. 'Please tell me. I won't be bored.'

He looked down at her hand, making her conscious of her impulsiveness, and hastily she withdrew it. How awful it was, having to think before she did anything because of this submerged tension between them that just about anything could bring bubbling to the surface.

To her surprise, he retrieved her hand and held it for a few reassuring moments before he let it fall again. Sheona felt less of a fool, but more bewildered than ever. What an unpredictable man he was. She never knew where she stood with him. Was that what intrigued her so much about him? Their relationship was all spice and then, when the spice became too sharp, he sweetened it with sugar.

It frightened her, how she was developing a taste for a spicy relationship occasionally laced with sugar.

'I believe you meant that,' he said, after what seemed immeasurable moments.

Meant what? she wondered frantically. Her wandering thoughts had made her lose the thread of the con-

versation. Then she remembered she'd said she wouldn't
be bored if he told her about the perfume. 'I did mean
it,' she assured him.

'Getting interested against your will?' he teased with
a lightness that invited her to smile with him.

'Sickening, isn't it?' she teased back.

'For you, maybe, but not for me. I've had this plan
in my mind for years, waiting for the right moment—
and that moment's now. You see, when my mother
launched Love she was way ahead of her time. It was a
"green" product and untested on animals when very few
people cared about such things. She circulated it among
her friends, and built up a market by word of mouth,
but it's always been limited. Consequently, it's never
made a profit or even broken even. The losses have been
absorbed by other family businesses.'

'Drummond Advertising and Drummond Island?'
Sheona put in thoughtfully.

'What do you know about Drummond Island?' he
asked, his dark eyebrows rising in surprise.

'Only the little Cordelia told me,' she admitted. 'She
thought if I knew more of your background we might
get along better.'

'The eternal optimist,' Marcus replied, then continued, 'Anyway, I've modernised production to cope
with world-wide demand, changed the perfume's name,
and put all the expertise of my advertising agency into
its promotion. The TV commercials will be backed by
poster and newspaper advertising, and Shireen and her
co-star are contracted to do promotional chat shows and
so on.'

Sheona absorbed that, and commented, 'You really
weren't exaggerating, then, when you said you had
millions tied up in this campaign. But why risk so much
if you already have successful businesses?'

'My mother believed in the perfume. So do I, and I also believe in diversifying. If the perfume is successful other organic cosmetics she pioneered can be added to the range. The prospects are limitless.'

Was that business talk to cover an act of love for a mother who'd died while he was so young? Sheona sneaked a reassessing glance at him. Impossible to tell. Marcus's face gave nothing away.

'The commercials will tell an ongoing story,' he continued, definitely all business now.

'Like episodes in a romantic serial?' she guessed.

'You've got it. This one exploits the idea that there are basically two kinds of women—the practical kind and the eternal female. In a fraught situation like a shipwreck, the practical woman will grab her passport. The eternal female will grab her perfume.'

'And there's no prize for spotting which one we're with,' Sheona commented.

'None at all.'

'Well, I'm the other sort,' Sheona told him bluntly. 'I'd definitely grab my passport.'

'Then you're ripe for conversion,' Marcus replied in that silky way that sent shivers down her spine. Before she could think of a snappy answer he beamed on the video.

They were transported to the Indian Ocean. A yacht was on fire and Shireen was in a cabin, magnificently suntanned and magnificently beautiful in a bikini that was just this side of decent. She was running her hands swiftly over her most prized possessions. Diamonds, pearls—and, of course her passport and perfume. Then she grabbed the perfume, thrust it into the cleavage of her bikini-top and dived out of the window into the blue, blue sea.

The scene cut to Shireen being washed up on the white sand of a palm-ringed tropical island, close to the muscled legs of a man standing astride in the receding surf. Sheona expected to see more of him but she was disappointed. The camera stayed with Shireen, who glanced up at him, then sat up languidly. Looking all the more magnificent for her soaking, she calmly took the perfume from her cleavage and lifted her wet hair to dab it on her neck. A muscled arm came down, the hand outstretched to take hers and lift her to her feet.

And that was it, except that a voice-over intoned, 'If you want to make a man a slave, use...' and a picture of a bottle of perfume with 'Slave' emblazoned on it filled the screen.

The video ended, and Sheona, who had been enthralled against her will, exclaimed, 'What a tease! What does he look like...the man with the hunky body?'

Marcus smiled. 'That's just the reaction we want. The hero's identity will be a closely guarded secret until the next episode so that the commercial has it all—drama, glamour, sex and suspense. The idea behind this first episode is that every woman will identify with the heroine, add her own ideal man and then rush out and buy the perfume to enslave him.'

'Clever...' Sheona admitted. She hadn't wanted to be grabbed by the commercial, and yet she had been. When that strong masculine hand had reached down she'd actually felt as though she were there to take it, and she was sure her reaction had nothing to do with Shireen being her twin. No...she'd been romanced, almost seduced, into projecting herself into the commercial by the music, the breathtaking setting and the story. And there was more to it than that, as well...

As if he were telepathic, Marcus asked, 'Which man did you imagine was reaching down for you?'

'Mel Gibson,' she lied, fighting down a rush of colour that made her feel hot and breathless. She couldn't tell this moody man sitting beside her on the bed that *he'd* been the hero she'd projected into the commercial. She was still trying to come to terms with that herself.

Marcus fixed smouldering brown eyes on her. 'I shouldn't think you'll be alone in that, but if you had a real man in your life you wouldn't need to fantasise quite so wildly.'

'What's wrong with being wild once in a while?' she retorted with a flippancy she was far from feeling. 'I'm normally so tame in my quiet little life that even I'm aware of my high boredom factor.'

'You've never bored me,' he replied abruptly.

Sheona was breathless all over again. She waited for more, but apparently he'd said all he was willing to, and embarrassment at the lengthening silence made her add shyly, 'I thought I had. Several times.'

'No.' His denial was brief but it meant everything to Sheona. It made her hope that perhaps she'd actually been out of Shireen's shadow long enough to develop a real personality of her own. That had always been vital to her, but it seemed even more important now.

'Have I ever bored you?' Marcus shot the question at her in the lethally unexpected way he so often had.

Unprepared, she blurted out, 'No.'

'Then perhaps there's hope for us yet.'

'What do you mean?' she asked, hoping he wouldn't think she was fishing for things he'd rather leave unsaid— even though she was.

After an infinitesimal pause he replied, 'I mean we got off on the wrong foot and we've been out of step ever since. Mostly I think we're doomed to stay that way but sometimes...just sometimes, I think maybe we're not.'

Sheona wasn't any the wiser, but she was afraid to question him more closely. Deep down she knew that, whatever answers he gave, she wasn't ready for them. Somehow, with the minimum of effort, Marcus was able to keep her in a state of total confusion. Every time she tried to clarify the situation she only ended up more confused than ever.

She risked another look at his face. It didn't exactly invite further confidences. She was baffled by this habit he had of shutting her out whenever she seemed to be getting close to him. After all, he was the one who'd advocated the advantages of a good working relationship.

But if she'd learned anything about this unpredictable man she'd learned that work was as safe a subject as they were ever likely to find—from his point of view, anyway. With that in mind she asked, 'What happens in the next commercial?'

'The heroine discovers the man who's rescued her is living with his own harem like some kind of king on the island. She sizes up the opposition and reaches for her perfume again. In the third and final episode, all the other girls are piled into a launch and deported while she remains on the island as its undisputed queen.'

Sheona smiled and murmured, 'The stuff that dreams are made of...'

'That's what it's all about,' he agreed.

And what, she wondered, are you all about, Marcus Drummond? What's your particular fantasy? She was studying the chiselled planes of his face, the firm lips, the aggressive jut of his jaw, trying to come to some positive conclusion about that, when somewhere in the distance a doorbell pealed.

Marcus got up off the bed, strode over to the video and ejected the tape. 'That will be Jason Huston,' he said.

'Who?' She'd never wanted to be alone with Marcus, but now she found she didn't particularly want to share him with anybody else, either. *What the blazes was happening to her?*

'Jason is the male model in the commercials,' Marcus explained. 'We make an early start for Drummond Island tomorrow so he's spending the night here. I'd like you to meet him but if you'd rather wait until the morning...?'

It wasn't particularly late and, besides, being with Marcus had stimulated her to the point where she was wide awake. 'Give me a few minutes and I'll be down,' she decided.

'That's my girl.'

Marcus left her with a warmth that had nothing to do with the heat of outrage that had fired her body when he'd strode unasked into her bedroom. His girl, indeed, though! What a joke, except that he'd sounded decidedly friendly as he'd said it.

Sheona was smiling to herself as she rapidly brushed out her drying hair and threw back on the clothes she'd worn for dinner. She had a quick glance in the mirror, then paused to take a more objective look at herself. No doubt about it, she had a special glow that hadn't been there before.

She almost blushed as she realised it had nothing to do with meeting the man whose muscular arms and legs had appeared in the video. No, her eyes, her skin, everything about her, were glowing at the prospect of being with Marcus again.

And yet Marcus himself wasn't exactly what she'd call the stuff that dreams were made of. He was too unpredictable, too autocratic—almost too much of a man. Only a woman he loved would be able to manage him.

A woman he loved...

Her thoughts faltered there. It wasn't quite safe to couple Marcus with love. It put wild thoughts into her head. Silly thoughts. It made her forget that the brief interludes when he was nice to her scarcely made up for the times when he treated her abominably.

If it ever came to a reckoning he had a lot to answer for in plucking her from her safe retreat and plunging her into his world with all its uncertainties and seductive glamour. But would there ever be a reckoning between herself and Marcus? She doubted it. When his use for her was over he'd drop her smartly back where he'd found her, and that would be it.

And a good thing, too, she told herself sternly. Her glow was still with her, though, as she picked up the tray he'd forgotten and carried it downstairs. She took it into the kitchen and put it on a counter by the sink. She paused to remember herself and Marcus here such a short while ago... the domesticity... the rage...

The room seemed empty without him. Safe, when she'd lost her taste for being safe...

'I thought I heard you,' Marcus said. 'I also thought I'd better come to fetch you. I wouldn't want you getting lost.'

Sheona spun round. He was leaning nonchalantly against the door-frame, looking devilishly handsome, devilishly dangerous. She felt unsafe again—and happy. She could feel the life and vitality generated by his closeness bubbling through her veins, parting her lips into a welcoming smile.

'You look quite devastating when you smile like that,' Marcus murmured, and seemed surprised that he'd said such a thing.

'You mean I look like Shireen?' she asked, just the tiniest catch in her voice.

'No, I don't mean that at all. You might be identical twins, but at certain times you're unmistakably different.'

'Is that good?'

'It's a fact.'

Sheona had been fishing for compliments again, but he wasn't co-operating. Funny how she, who despised flattery, suddenly couldn't get enough of it. From

Marcus, anyway. Unfortunately there was no reason for him to stroke her ego in earnest until he got her before the cameras and needed to hype her up. And then it would all be embarrassingly false, while just now he'd actually sounded sincere.

'Why so sulky all of a sudden?' Marcus asked, his eyes narrowing as he noticed the sudden droop of her full lips.

'I'm not sulky, I'm thoughtful,' she bluffed.

'Don't frighten Jason with thoughts,' he advised with a slight smile. 'He's a really nice chap but he's heavier on brawn than brains. Just try to react to the brawn. That will make him happy, and hopefully it will stir up some chemistry that will be good for the cameras. Frankly, he's no Mel Gibson in the acting department, but Shireen's so good that she can carry him. With you, however——'

'Don't depress me with the "however",' Sheona broke in. 'I'm still banking on Shireen turning up in time to save me. Still, I liked Jason's body in the video, and if his hand had reached down for me I'd have grabbed it.'

'No kidding?' Marcus asked, looking amused.

'No kidding,' she affirmed, wanting him to know he wasn't the only male who could get a positive reaction out of her.

'I'll remember that,' he murmured, smiling in a way she didn't quite understand as he took her arm and led her out of the kitchen.

Sheona was very conscious of his touch, and missed it as he let go of her arm in the passage. Her shoulder brushed against his as they turned into another passage, and she was very conscious of that, too. Deliberately she moved further away, afraid that his acute perception would pick up the way she was feeling. Marcus glanced down at her but said nothing, which wasn't much like him.

She felt unsure of herself again, as though he were the one who had distanced himself from her. It made her realise how much her confidence rose when she felt she had his approval, and she was annoyed with herself. She didn't have time to dwell on it, though, because he was opening a door and standing back for her to enter.

She found herself in a large room full of well-worn armchairs and sofas. She was surprised, expecting a smart, designer layout, but this was obviously a family room that had evolved over the generations with comfort rather than style in mind. The October evening was chill and a log fire burned cosily in the hearth, offering a welcome she couldn't resist. She relaxed again, feeling instantly at home as she made her way to the fire.

'Sheona, meet Jason,' Marcus said as a hefty young man rose clumsily to his feet from the depths of a floral armchair.

He had a shock of fair hair, paralysingly blue eyes and a face that was unbelievably handsome. The perfect foil for Shireen's dark beauty, Sheona thought involuntarily, but he might just as well have been chiselled out of marble for all the sexual effect he had on her.

She could understand that other women would flip their lids over him, though—those who hadn't first met Marcus.

That thought brought a slight blush to her cheeks and she didn't notice that Marcus, studying her reaction intently, frowned. All Sheona was conscious of was that, feeling no attraction for Jason, she could react entirely naturally towards him. She held out her hand and said pleasantly, 'Hello, Jason. I've just been watching a video of the first commercial. I'm sure it will be a great success.'

'I've seen it but I'm not in it,' Jason replied, shaking her hand with care. 'I'm hired for the sequels, when my face will be seen. I was working on another commercial when the first one was made, so somebody else's body was used.'

'Oh.' Sheona turned her face towards Marcus and asked, 'Whose?'

'Mine,' he replied, and smiled.

Blushing fiercely as she remembered what she'd said, she groaned, 'I want to die. I just want to die.'

'I thought you would,' Marcus replied. And he laughed, an unexpectedly carefree sound that swept away her embarrassment and had her laughing with him.

'I'm always saying the wrong thing to you,' she sighed eventually.

'That makes two of us,' he breathed, the laughter dying from his eyes but a warmth remaining.

Sheona felt strangely breathless again.

'Have I missed something?' Jason asked, blinking at them in a confused way.

Both Marcus and Sheona turned to him and said together, 'No.'

They exchanged an involuntary look that lingered longer than it should have done, then Marcus went over to the drinks cabinet. Sheona's eyes wanted to stay with him and it took a very real effort to force them back to Jason.

She sat down by the fire, but when it became obvious that Jason had nothing further to add she said chattily, 'You must be upset Shireen's vanished, but I'm sure she won't miss the filming. I shouldn't think you'll be landed with me for long.'

'I can't see that it will make much difference,' Jason surprised her by replying. 'You look like two peas in a pod to me.'

'But you must have noticed we're nothing alike in personality!' she exclaimed, even more surprised.

'I've never met Shireen,' Jason replied placidly. 'I haven't been in the business long and this is the first time we've been teamed together. I just know her from her work, and if Marcus hadn't explained you're her twin I'd have thought you were her.'

'Well, I'm not, which will become painfully obvious when the cameras start rolling,' Sheona warned him. 'I'm not much good as a model.'

'Why?' Jason asked, his blue eyes opening wide. 'You just do what the director tells you to do, and that's all there is to it.'

Sheona felt a stirring of irritation, but she smothered it. Jason was obviously immune to atmosphere when something wasn't going right, so he wasn't likely to understand somebody like herself who was particularly sensitive to disapproval. She didn't think she'd get far if she tried to point out the difference in their temperaments, though, so she just said mildly, 'I'll try to remember that if the going gets rough.'

'I'll help you,' he assured her kindly. 'I'll help Shireen, too, if she needs it.'

'Thank you.' Sheona avoided Marcus's eyes. She didn't think it right to be sharing secret amusement with him. Jason might not be very bright, but his heart was in the right place.

He relapsed into another heavy silence and she was glad when Marcus intervened to ask, 'What will you have to drink, Sheona?'

'A spritzer, please.'

Was that another special smile Marcus gave her as he handed her a tall glass of white wine mixed with lemonade and ice? She smiled back but she was puzzled, unable to fathom out why they were suddenly so relaxed together. Then she realised that she and Marcus were no longer reacting to each other like strangers. Against all the odds, a familiarity had developed between them that was almost like—friendship.

She was so startled that she didn't hear Jason asking Marcus for mineral water, then explaining to her, 'I never touch alcohol. I have to look after the body and the looks. I don't smoke or stay up late, either.'

'Pardon?' she asked blankly, becoming aware that both men were looking at her, expecting some kind of reaction.

Jason patiently repeated what he'd said. She murmured a suitable reply and both she and Marcus did little more than listen while he talked on for half an hour about the two things that really interested him—his diet and his exercise routine.

He almost became animated but Sheona had too much on her mind to pay much attention, and she suspected that Marcus wasn't listening very closely, either. Sometimes she was aware of him watching her. Sometimes she watched him when she thought it was safe to do so. And sometimes their eyes met. Then they would both smile, and the strange glow she was beginning to associate with having Marcus close to her would burn with extra warmth.

Regret spiked through her when Jason ran out of conversation, stood up, and said very firmly that he was going to bed.

'Me, too,' she endorsed, not wanting to put the novelty of feeling comfortable with Marcus to the test by remaining alone with him.

They all walked up the stairs together, Marcus showing Jason to his room first, then walking further down the passage with her. 'An early call tomorrow, I'm afraid,' he said softly. 'Five o'clock. We leave at six.'

'I'll be ready,' she promised, shy again now that Jason was no longer there to act as a buffer between them.

'Thank you for being nice to Jason.'

'It wasn't hard. He's a nice person.'

'So are you,' Marcus said. He tipped her face up to his, dropped an unexpectedly gentle kiss on her forehead, and went away.

CHAPTER SEVEN

IT WAS the gentleness of Marcus's kiss that kept Sheona wakeful that night. Hour after restless hour she puzzled over the complexity of a man who could infuriate her one moment and charm her the next. She'd never known anybody like him before. She was very sure she never would again.

But, temporarily, control of her life had passed from her hands to his, and she had to get on with it. She couldn't help wishing, though, that she'd never met him at all. Then she wouldn't be wakeful like this, wondering how close his bedroom was to hers, and whether he was unable to rest, too.

His image was before her eyes when she finally fell asleep, and it seemed only moments later that his hand was on her shoulder, shaking her awake.

'Sheona.' Marcus, wearing a scarlet dressing-gown over black silk pyjamas, spoke her name softly, making it sound like a caress.

She groaned in an anguish that seemed to come from her soul, half believing this was another feverish dream. It was all too much, and she flung herself away from his tantalising touch, burrowing her head under the pillow to block out all sight and sound of him.

The bed depressed on one side as he sat down on it. 'Are you always this surly in the morning?' he asked.

He sounded wide awake and teasing, two things that were a crime against humanity in her present shattered state. 'Go away,' she muttered huskily, feeling like death warmed up.

Marcus flung away the quilt, seized her up in his arms and strode into the bathroom with her. For a few moments she was too shocked to protest, then she squealed in disbelief as he dumped her unceremoniously in the shower.

'Good morning, Sheona,' he said, and turned the tap full on.

She gasped as water gushed over her, drenching her nightgown so that its full folds shrank to the shape of her shocked body. 'How dare you?' she spluttered, turning from him as she reached blindly and instinctively for the tap. Only this wasn't her shower and the tap wasn't where it should have been.

'Breakfast in fifteen minutes,' Marcus told her briskly. 'Be there, or I'll come and get you.'

'I hate you!' she screamed, but he only laughed and went away.

Sheona finally found the tap and the gush of water mercifully ceased. She was wide awake now. Furiously awake. If she could have got her hands on Marcus she would have murdered him. As it was, she seethed with frustration.

Her soaked nightgown clung to her but she eventually managed to strip it off. She kicked it viciously into a corner of the shower, but that did little to ease her feelings. So he thought this was funny, did he? The man had a warped sense of humour!

Rebelliously she felt like locking herself in the bathroom, but if she'd learned anything in her dealings with Marcus it was caution. If he hadn't thought twice about dumping her in the shower he wasn't likely to hesitate at knocking down the door... and she had no clothes on.

Fifteen minutes was what he'd given her, and fifteen minutes was undoubtedly what he meant! If she wasn't ready it would only give him an excuse to get physical again.

Get physical again... With a quiver that was somewhere between a thrill and a shudder she grabbed a towel and shifted herself. Really shifted. Within less than the specified time she'd re-packed—except for the soaked nightie that still lay in mute protest on the shower floor—and had dressed in an exotically flowered trouser suit fashioned from uncrushable silk. Its brilliant citrus colours were a bit hard to take at this time in the morning but its lightness and loose smock-like top made it comfortable for travelling.

Sheona was sitting at the dressing-table trying to blow-dry her hair and file a chipped fingernail at the same time when Marcus walked back in on her after no more than a cursory knock on the door. He was wearing cream trousers and a cream shirt with box pockets and epaulettes.

She thought he looked sexy enough to be co-starring in the commercial. It was a shameful thought and she banished it hastily.

'You're two minutes early,' she complained, glaring at him.

'I thought you might be sulking and in need of further prompting,' he replied, unashamedly studying her from top to toe.

'Any more prompting from you and you'll have to carry me kicking and screaming on to the plane,' she threatened, wishing he wouldn't look at her like that. It made her feel move quivery than she already was.

His eyebrows quirked in amusement. 'Do you think I wouldn't?'

She knew damn well that he would so she sniffed disdainfully and turned a huffy shoulder on him. Marcus wasn't in the least deterred. He strolled over to her, took the drier from her hand and played the warm air over her hair. He seemed to make a caress of that, too, and Sheona found the intimacy of his action more devastating than if he'd taken her into his arms.

Well, almost.

He was acting like a lover who took it as his right to help her get ready, and, strangely enough, that was how she felt, too. She was so stunned by his behaviour, and her acceptance of it, that she felt forced to pretend that none of it was happening. She picked up her emery board and bent her head over her damaged nail, filing away at it as though it were the most important thing on her mind right then.

She hoped he was deceived.

He lifted her long, heavy hair from her neck, letting strands fall through his fingers as they dried. Sheona sat absolutely still when the repair to her nail was finished, mesmerised by the feel of his fingers in her hair, speechless at the sheer seductive luxury of a man like Marcus performing a service like this for her.

All the rage, hostility and resentment drained from her, to be replaced by completely opposite feelings. It seemed to her that in these silent, sensual moments she and Marcus were closer than they'd ever been.

Inevitably, their eyes met in the dressing-table mirror.

His were so inscrutable that hers took on a childlike bewilderment, almost a childlike hurt.

'Don't look at me like that,' he said roughly.

'Like what?' she whispered, really hurt now. It was so unfair that whatever she was feeling was reflected in her eyes, whereas his showed nothing at all—unless it was anger.

'It doesn't matter.' Marcus put the drier down on the dressing-table and turned from her in one of his abrupt, decisive movements. 'We're late enough for breakfast as it is.'

'And that's my fault, I suppose?' she asked bitterly, her sense of let-down making her feel strangely defeated as she rose to her feet.

'It doesn't matter whose fault it is, it's a fact.'

'There are times, Marcus Drummond, when I can live without you and your damned facts!' She stalked ahead of him to the door, got through it and slammed it in his face.

They had nothing to say to each other at breakfast, and Jason kept up a monologue about his early-morning work-out and his regret that it was too early and too dark for his usual morning jog. Both men ate steak and eggs while Sheona nibbled toast. She didn't feel like eating anything at all but she didn't want Marcus to realise how deeply he'd upset her. He should definitely be a model, she thought. He certainly knew how to switch it on and off!

The housekeeper, whom Marcus introduced as Elaine, was a tall, friendly woman in her mid-forties, but she didn't help matters by mistaking Sheona for Shireen. Marcus swiftly put her right, and Sheona had to smile through her exclamations of how alike she and her twin were.

In actual fact, Sheona had never felt less like smiling. Everything Elaine said reinforced her own view that Marcus, too, sometimes forgot which twin she was. Although he was furious with Shireen, that might only be on a business level. Personally, he might be feeling very differently. That would explain his tender moments, when his longing for Shireen got the better of him and she, Sheona, just happened to be there.

After all, Shireen was obviously no stranger to his breakfast table. That told its own story.

A lump formed in Sheona's throat, making it impossible for her to swallow any more unwanted toast.

'Are you finished?' Marcus was looking from his watch to her and Jason. 'The cab will be here in fifteen minutes.'

Sheona nodded, avoiding his gaze. In future she wasn't going to look or speak to him unless it was absolutely essential. It would be just too embarrassing to be caught with her heart hanging out of her eyes again.

It was a nine-hour private-charter flight, but the Seychelles were four hours ahead of British time and it was late evening when they landed on Mahe, the largest of the many islands scattered like gleaming emeralds over a sapphire and turquoise sea.

Sheona, though, had never been in a mood so far removed from enchantment. She had a deep core of misery within her that she couldn't come to terms with, or even understand.

Marcus had worked throughout the entire flight on the papers in the two bulging briefcases he'd brought with him. Sheona had remained determined to have nothing to do with him, and yet it hurt that he was equally determined to have nothing to do with her.

I'm in deep trouble, she thought, and tried to convince herself that mutual rejection was as good a way out of it as any.

Her head believed it, but her heart mourned...

'Drummond Island has no airstrip,' Marcus said as the jet taxied along the runway. 'We'll stay overnight on Mahe and travel on in the morning.'

Jason was yawning too much to answer and Sheona only nodded, trying not to yawn as well. She'd had no real sleep since yesterday, and had only picked at the food offered to her during the flight.

Marcus's dark eyes fixed on her. 'You look dreadful,' he said.

She felt dreadful, but it wasn't what she wanted to hear, and so she didn't answer.

'Dinner in your room and straight to bed,' he ordered, but Sheona didn't flatter herself that his concern went deeper than her looks. Cameras could be so cruel to a girl not looking her best. He probably had a double interest, anyway. If she was confined to her room that neatly spared him from having to entertain her for what was left of the evening.

Well, that suited her, didn't it?

But she was feeling decidedly sulky as well as weary as a waiting car whisked them to a palm-shaded beach hotel where Marcus personally conducted her to her room. It hurt that he was so anxious to get rid of her. She wished it didn't, but it did.

'No need to unpack much,' he told her, going back to the door. 'We make another early start tomorrow. Relax and shower while I arrange the meal. Half an hour suit you?'

She nodded and sank on to one of the twin beds, loosening the straps on her sandals and kicking them off. Here she was, in one of the most exotic locations in the world, and all she was interested in was the man who'd just left her. She could only suppose that lack of food and sleep was making her delirious.

Dejectedly she looked around the room. It was simply but pleasantly furnished, cool with air-conditioning, and when she mustered up enough energy to investigate she found she had her own bathroom, and her own balcony overlooking a lagoon.

She leaned on the balcony for a while, trying to imagine she was just another holidaymaker with no worries or cares, and nothing to do but enjoy herself. There was a burst of laughter from somewhere along the beach and the lightest of breezes carried with it the appetising aroma of barbecued meat.

IT'S FUN! IT'S FREE!
AND IT COULD MAKE YOU A
MILLIONAIRE

If you've ever played scratch-off lottery tickets, you should be familiar with how our games work. On each of the first four tickets (numbered 1 to 4 in the upper right) there are Pink Metallic Strips to scratch off.

Using a coin, do just that—carefully scratch the PINK strips to reveal how much each ticket could be worth if it is a winning ticket. Tickets could be worth from $100.00 to $1,000,000.00 in lifetime money.

Note, also, that each of your 4 tickets has a unique sweepstakes Lucky Number . . . and that's 4 chances for a **BIG WIN!**

FREE BOOKS!

At the same time you play your tickets for big prizes, you are invited to play ticket #5 for the chance to get one or more free books from Harlequin®. We give away free books to introduce readers to the benefits of the Harlequin Reader Service®.

Accepting the free book(s) places you under no obligation to buy anything! You may keep your free book(s) and return the accompanying statement marked "cancel." But if we don't hear from you, then every month, we'll deliver 6 of the newest Harlequin Romance® novels right to your door. You'll pay the low subscriber price of just $2.24* each plus 25¢ delivery and applicable sales tax, if any*. That's the complete price, and compared to cover price of $2.89 each in stores—quite a bargain!

Of course, you may play "THE BIG WIN" without requesting any free book(s) by scratching tickets #1 through #4 only. But remember, that first shipment of one or more books is FREE!

PLUS A FREE GIFT!

One more thing, when you accept the free book(s) on ticket #5, you are also entitled to play ticket #6, which is GOOD FOR A GREAT GIFT! Like the book(s), this gift is totally free and yours to keep as thanks for giving our Reader Service a try!

So scratch off the PINK STRIPS on all your BIG WIN tickets and send for everything today! You've got nothing to lose and everything to gain!

Here are your BIG WIN Game Tickets, potentially worth from $100.00 to $1,000,000.00 each. Scratch off the PINK METALLIC STRIP on each of your Sweepstakes tickets to see what you could win and mail your entry right away. (SEE OFFICIAL RULES IN BACK OF BOOK FOR DETAILS!)

This could be your lucky day - GOOD LUCK!

TICKET 1
Scratch PINK METALLIC STRIP to reveal potential value of this ticket if it is a winning ticket. Return all game tickets intact.

LUCKY NUMBER

7J 160721

TICKET 2
Scratch PINK METALLIC STRIP to reveal potential value of this ticket if it is a winning ticket. Return all game tickets intact.

LUCKY NUMBER

3L 160721

TICKET 3
Scratch PINK METALLIC STRIP to reveal potential value of this ticket if it is a winning ticket. Return all game tickets intact.

LUCKY NUMBER

9Y 160721

TICKET 4
Scratch PINK METALLIC STRIP to reveal potential value of this ticket if it is a winning ticket. Return all game tickets intact.

LUCKY NUMBER

1K 160721

TICKET 5
We're giving away brand new books to selected individuals. Scratch PINK METALLIC STRIP for number of free books you will receive.

AUTHORIZATION CODE

130107-742

TICKET 6
We have an outstanding added gift for you if you are accepting our free books. Scratch PINK METALLIC STRIP to reveal gift.

AUTHORIZATION CODE

130107-742

YES! Enter my Lucky Numbers in THE BIG WIN Sweepstakes, and when winners are selected, tell me if I've won any prize. If PINK METALLIC STRIP is scratched off on ticket #5, I will also receive one or more FREE Harlequin Romance® novels along with the FREE GIFT on ticket #6, as explained on the opposite page.

116 CIH AH2A (U-H-R-01/93)

NAME _____

ADDRESS _____ APT. _____

CITY _____ STATE _____ ZIP CODE _____

Book offer limited to one per household and not valid to current Harlequin Romance® subscribers. All orders subject to approval.
© 1991 HARLEQUIN ENTERPRISES LIMITED.   PRINTED IN U.S.A.

FOLD AND DETACH ALONG THIS DOTTED LINE—RETURN ALL GAME TICKETS INTACT.

Carefully detach card along dotted lines and mail today!
Play all your BIG WIN tickets and get everything you're
entitled to—including FREE BOOKS and a FREE GIFT!

ALTERNATE MEANS OF ENTRY: Print your name and address on a 3" × 5" piece
of plain paper and send to: Harlequin Reader Service®, 3010 Walden Ave.,
P.O. Box 1867, Buffalo, NY 14269-1867. Limit: One entry per envelope.

She felt remote from it all, and her eyes drifted to a line of water gleaming whitely in the moonlight where the ocean fretted against the reef that protected the lagoon.

How idyllic it all was—except that Marcus wished she was Shireen.

Annoyed with her own dejection, she tried to shower some life and enthusiasm back into herself, but the minute the water gushed over her she remembered Marcus thrusting her into the shower that morning.

He'd laughed—and what a fool she'd been not to laugh with him. Everything might have been so different then. So very different.

Sheona sighed, a tiny sound that seemed to come straight from her suffering heart. Then she froze as though the warm refreshing water had suddenly turned to ice. Now she knew what was the matter with her.

She'd tumbled helplessly and hopelessly in love with a man she should, if she were in her right mind, detest. But she wasn't in her right mind—hadn't been since he'd stormed into her home and carried his conquest straight through her defences to her heart!

As if that wasn't bad enough, she couldn't even try to win his heart in return. She'd never know whether she'd captured it or not. Marcus was already using her as a model substitute for Shireen. She could just as easily become a substitute for love as well!

What on earth was she going to do? And how strange it was that her cheeks could burn so hotly while the rest of her body felt as though it were carved out of ice. Not in her wildest dreams had she imagined that love could be as swift, chaotic and confusing as this!

One thought grew in her mind, dominating all others: Marcus *mustn't* know she loved him.

As long as she could keep her secret she should somehow manage to bluff her way through until Shireen returned and made escape from him possible. So, whatever happened, Marcus must not even suspect how she felt about him.

That resolution gave Sheona a sense of purpose that she could hang on to like a lifeline. Her panic subsided and she regained her self-control. She even mocked herself, muttering aloud that it wasn't possible to fall in love in such a short space of time, and that being in the tropics must have boiled her brains.

Infatuated with Marcus, perhaps. In love—no!

She wrapped herself in a towel and went into the bedroom, fishing out of her baggage a flowing multi-coloured house-robe that almost looked like an evening gown but was hedonistically comfortable.

She was startled when a knock sounded at the door, and turned her head quickly towards it, expecting Marcus to enter in his usual cavalier fashion. Nothing happened, except that the knock sounded again.

Not Marcus, then. He'd never be so formal. It must be the waiter with the food. She grabbed the robe and fled back to the bathroom, calling, 'Please come in and leave the meal. I won't be a minute.'

She was rather longer than that, slipping on the robe and unpinning the chignon she'd fashioned her hair into for coolness's sake when she'd felt sticky and weary during the flight. Then she brushed her hair and tied it back loosely with the thin sash of the robe she was wearing, letting the long ends dangle down her back.

'You look a new woman.'

Marcus.

His words greeted her as she went into the bedroom, causing her to check involuntarily. Surprise, anticipation, excitement and dread were among the jumble of emotions that shivered through her, rapidly followed by a flood of love it took all her will-power to suppress.

He saw the shiver and frowned. 'There's no need to look at me as if I'm some kind of monster.'

'I've always thought a bedroom was a private place,' she retorted with a coolness she was far from feeling. 'You obviously have different ideas.'

'I haven't come here to quarrel with you. I've come to make sure you eat properly. You've hardly touched a thing all day.'

'I didn't think you noticed.'

'I noticed.'

Marcus came towards her and she felt an inner weakness that turned her to jelly beneath her poised exterior. He looked more handsome than he'd any right to be, in a white shirt and jacket teamed with dark trousers. She thought he must have just showered, too, because some tendrils of dark hair were clinging damply to his forehead.

Sheona inhaled the fresh manly smell of him and longed to reach up and brush those tendrils back. The urge was so strong that she was only able to resist it by clenching her hands into fists.

Marcus noticed that, too. 'You're still too tense,' he said, and almost shattered her calm façade by taking her hands and gently unclenching each fist in turn. Then he raised her slender palms to his lips and kissed them. His eyes met hers over them. He smiled and added softly, 'Just to prove I'm not a monster all the time.'

His touch, the imprint of his lips on her sensitive palms, weakened her so much that she could only feel relieved—wistfully relieved—when he let her hands fall, took her arm, and with another smile led her out on to the balcony.

Marcus, please don't smile at me like that, she pleaded silently. Just be your normal horrid self. Give me another reason to start hating you again. I need one so desperately!

But Marcus wouldn't co-operate. When he chose to charm he charmed in earnest. 'Your dinner awaits, *madame*,' he intoned, adding a lilt of humour to the usual waiter's line.

Sheona caught her breath. A table had been set out on the balcony. There were covered dishes and champagne on ice—and two chairs. 'Jason?' she questioned involuntarily.

'He's at the hotel's evening barbecue eating his usual half an ox,' Marcus replied, holding out a chair for her.

So he hadn't confined her to her room to be rid of her, after all! She could stop sulking, start living a little—if she dared.

In an almost trance-like state, Sheona allowed herself to be seated. She wasn't at all sure she could cope with a moonlight dinner tête-à-tête with Marcus. It would have been hard enough in Bournemouth, but here, under tropical stars, with the Indian Ocean sighing against the beach just a few short feet away—no, she couldn't be expected to cope with that and still keep a cool head on her shoulders!

Except that she had to.

She had to admit that Marcus made it easy for her. He talked lightly and fascinatingly about the islands as they dined on melon, followed by reef fish baked in palm leaves and served with savoury rice. She drank one glass of champagne and he didn't try to press more on her when she refused another.

'Granite?' she questioned when he told her the granite on the islands, which were some thousand miles from the African coast, proved that India had once been joined with Africa. 'I haven't seen any granite.'

'You haven't seen anything yet, but you will,' he replied. 'Tonight you just need to rest. You were looking absolutely shattered by the time we arrived.'

'I felt absolutely shattered,' she admitted, 'and that's no good for a model, is it?'

'It's no good for anyone. Especially you.'

'Why especially me?' she asked, surprised.

'You look healthy enough normally but you have a sensitivity, almost a frailty, that makes you more vulnerable than most.'

Sheona was grateful for the moonlight, beguiling though it was. It meant he couldn't see the flush that rose to her cheeks at his perception. She'd had no idea he'd been studying her so closely or so acutely. She couldn't help feeling flattered, until she remembered it was important to him to keep her looking her best.

She felt deflated, and she took it as another caution not to confuse his business interest with a personal one. After all, his only purpose in pampering her like this was to make sure she relaxed properly. So what seemed romantic to her was just a ploy to him. To hide her true feelings she repeated lightly, 'Sensitive, frail and vulnerable—is that your way of saying I'm more trouble than Shireen?'

'Since you haven't run away, no.'

'There's not much chance of that now,' she replied, feeling even more deflated as a sudden guarded note in his voice brought all her worries and fears rushing back.

'No chance whatsoever,' he agreed.

That was his first show of ruthlessness since the meal began, and she thought it would be wise to change the subject. There was no sense in provoking him while she felt so weak emotionally. 'When's filming due to start?' she asked.

'Wednesday.'

Sheona put down her knife and fork in amazement. 'That's four days away! Why is it necessary for me and Jason to come out here so soon?'

'To get you acclimatised to the heat and get your skin colours the right tone before filming starts. I don't want either of you keeling over on the set. As for the suntan, there are artificial lotions, of course, but I want everything about these commercials to be authentic. No sense in spoiling the ship for a ha'p'orth of tar.'

'So that's what Shireen meant when she said to tell you her suntan's all right!' Sheona exclaimed. Then she smiled radiantly and repeated, 'Four more days! That means there's every chance she'll turn up before filming actually starts. Gosh, that makes me feel better. You don't know how much I was dreading going before the cameras.'

Marcus had finished his fish. He leaned back in his chair and surveyed her thoughtfully. 'Don't you think it's time you faced up to this phobia of yours? It's cramping your life.'

Sheona shook her head and put down her knife and fork, her own fish finished. 'My life is just the way I want it—or it was, until you hijacked me.'

'I see,' he replied with a wryness that puzzled her, but before she could question him he replaced her plate with an exotic concoction of pineapple, guava and mango. She began to eat, but almost against her will she heard herself voicing one of her biggest fears. 'Sometimes...just sometimes...I think you confuse me with Shireen.'

'I never confuse you with Shireen,' he replied positively.

'Most people do, one way or another.'

'Not me. Not in any way.'

'Oh.' Could she believe him? If she did it meant that when he was nice to her, when he kissed her, she wasn't just bathing in her sister's reflected glory. But why, if he wasn't recollecting he was with the wrong twin, did he always change so abruptly and become brutal again?

Sheona stole a look at his face, darkly handsome in the moonlight, and decided that no, these were questions she definitely couldn't ask him. They were too close to her heart and the secret it contained.

'Something's on your mind,' he said softly. 'Let's hear it. I don't like you frowning at me like that.'

She searched frantically for something she could ask that would steer her out of dangerous territory, but every thought she had was tied up with her infatuation for him. 'I was wondering...' she began slowly, waiting for inspiration to strike which, mercifully, it did '...what happened to your father. Cordelia told me about your mother but not about him.'

'Nothing much mattered to him after my mother died. I think he went looking for death. He found it somewhere close to the top of the Eiger. He was twenty years older than my mother and he was no mountaineer.'

'I'm sorry,' she said swiftly. Then, with her ready sympathy aroused, she added spontaneously, 'That must have been tough on you.'

'It was a long time ago.' Marcus's face twisted into an almost bitter smile. 'Drummond men have a reputation for falling in love late—and for life. I'm thirty-two. I guess the time is coming for me, too.'

There was an intensity in his eyes and voice that seemed to be concentrated entirely on her... so much so that she was almost overpowered. She found she was holding her breath, and her heart began to pound in a wild and wilful way.

'What do Murray women have a reputation for, Sheona?' he asked softly.

'I don't know,' she whispered.

'Then that's something else you have to find out about yourself,' he replied. 'I'm beginning to think you were meant to come to Drummond Island...'

CHAPTER EIGHT

THEY went to Drummond Island the next morning. A light plane took them to a neighbouring island, then they travelled on by launch, disembarking at a small pier protruding from a palm-fringed beach of fine white sand.

This morning Sheona was a different girl, rested and radiant, and enchanted with everything she saw. She was also still bemused from what Marcus had said last night. She'd yearned for him to explain more fully but he'd left her shortly afterwards, telling her brusquely to go straight to bed.

He'd softened his words, though, with another gentle kiss on her forehead. This time it hadn't kept her wakeful but had lulled her into the deep sleep she'd so desperately needed.

Now here they were on Drummond Island, where he was king and she was his captive. She smiled at her fanciful thoughts, and yet what had happened to her wasn't so very different from the scenario he'd mapped out for his commercials.

She was standing with Marcus as he loaded their baggage into the back of a mini-moke parked at the end of the pier, and she looked out to sea where the launch was powering its way to another island. The sound of its engine faded and everything was so peaceful, so unbelievably beautiful, that she felt she'd been cast adrift in the original Eden.

'Your island,' she breathed to Marcus, her eyes lifting to the gentle tree-covered hills that were all that remained of a mountain which had disappeared beneath the sea at the dawn of time. 'I don't know how you can bear to leave it.'

'I like the best of all worlds,' he replied, smiling at her awestruck expression.

Her eyes dropped to the spotless coral sand and she shook her head disbelievingly. 'I don't see how you can get better than this.'

'Perhaps not,' he admitted, 'but a man has to keep travelling until he finds what he wants.'

'What could you possibly want that isn't already here?'

He looked at her, his eyes blazing with a light that took her breath away. 'At the moment, nothing.'

Sheona almost gasped. He couldn't mean her, could he? No, of course not! She was letting the enchantment of this incredible jewel of an island carry her away.

Perhaps Marcus sensed her sudden tension because he turned away from her with one of his abrupt movements, and for once she wasn't sorry. It gave her time to recollect that her survival strategy didn't involve falling apart simply because she was with Marcus in a miniature paradise.

The problem was that strategy and the way she felt about him were far from compatible. Still, infatuation wasn't supposed to last for long, was it? It was only a transitory emotion, an illusion of love that lacked the staying power of the real thing.

She could be cured at any moment.

Sheona felt far from cured as Marcus's strong hand helped her into the front passenger-seat of the minimoke. He got behind the steering-wheel and tooted the horn to get the attention of Jason, who'd leapt out of the launch as soon as it had touched the pier and raced along the beach like an overgrown schoolboy just let out of class.

Jason came bounding back, grinning, and Sheona wondered mournfully why, if she'd had to fall for somebody, she couldn't have fallen for him. He had the classic blue-eyed fair-haired looks of a young god, and he was so uncomplicated.

She stole a look at Marcus, whose good looks were roughly chiselled rather than smoothly classic, and who was complex in the extreme. It all came down to charisma, she supposed. Marcus was loaded with it, while Jason had none. Not for her, anyway.

Jason got into the back with the luggage and looked so happy that she could only envy him. Now that Marcus was back on his own island he seemed to be distancing himself again. She didn't know why. She only knew that it hurt.

Marcus drove along a rough track that meandered through a little village of thatched chalets hidden from the beach by palm trees. An empty village. 'Where is everybody?' she asked.

'This is the tourist complex,' Marcus explained. 'It's empty because this is where the film crew will stay when they arrive on Tuesday.'

'Oh.' So the peace, the feeling of isolation, wouldn't last for long. All too soon, if Shireen delayed much longer, she would have to pose before the cameras—with Marcus's critical eyes upon her.

She couldn't do it. She knew she couldn't.

'We had tourists here when we shot the first commercial and it really didn't work,' Marcus went on. 'They followed us from location to location, getting in the way, slowing things down. We won't have that distraction this time.'

Sheona wondered whether it was only Mike Judson who'd actually got in the way, creating chaos between Marcus, his sister and Shireen. Whatever, he was obviously taking no chances this time.

The track wound past a long low building, its thatch extending to a wide veranda. 'What's that?' she asked.

'The restaurant and clubhouse,' Marcus explained. 'Naturally, we don't attract tourists who expect a lot of nightlife, but they like to socialise a bit in the evenings. We appeal to those who want a natural paradise, mostly divers—and honeymooners.'

'I can imagine,' she replied, her throat suddenly dry as her mind filled with a picture of honeymooning here with Marcus. She lapsed into self-conscious silence, then, afraid her silence was saying more than words might have done, she asked, 'Are there any Seychellois living here?'

'Of course. They work in the tourist complex, the cinnamon plantation or simply live off the land and the sea. A few go to Mahe, but most of them return. Francine, a Seychellois who manages the tourist business for me, spent a few years on Mahe but she didn't need too much persuading to come home. Her children are grown up now. They've chosen to stay and help her, and her mother looks after my house.'

'Sounds like a friendly set-up,' Sheona commented.

'The Seychelles are friendly islands.'

Marcus was driving up a hill through scented cinnamon groves, and Jason said in dismay, 'Aren't we staying close to the beach?'

'The house has its own beach. It's on the western side of the island, and the sunsets are pretty spectacular.'

'Any pirates' treasure?' Sheona asked whimsically.

'According to legend, yes, but I'd hate to have to find it. You could waste a lifetime looking for the treasure that's reputed to be buried in these islands.'

'I wouldn't mind having a shot at it,' Jason said enthusiastically from the back seat. 'If I found it I'd buy my own island.'

Sheona and Marcus smiled at each other in a brief moment of silent communication. Jason looked so much the man and yet really he was still a boy at heart. Marcus was the real man. She stirred in her seat as a new wave of love for him swept over her.

Marcus gave her another glance. 'Too hot?' he asked.

'No, nicely comfortable,' she fibbed, making it more realistic by adding, 'This breeze is a life-safer.'

'Make the most of it. Sea breezes are rare at this time of year when we're between monsoons.'

They dipped down a hill, climbed another, and as they were dipping again Marcus slowed almost to a stop while he rounded yet another bend. 'There it is,' he said. 'Home.'

Sheona caught her breath as she glimpsed a graceful two-storeyed colonial house that looked as though time had merged it into the landscape. It nestled amid a profusion of flowering bushes, palms and casuarina trees, whose strange jointed branches looked uncannily like horses' tails.

Wide verandas screened both storeys from the sun, the shutters at the french windows were open and welcoming, and so was the front door. The house stood at an angle so that it overlooked both its own beach and the one where they had landed, back down the incredibly green hills.

'It's perfect,' she breathed. 'Absolutely perfect.'

'Not sorry you came now?' Marcus asked, his lips parting in a smile that took her breath away again, a smile that seemed especially for her, and her alone.

Emotions she'd tried so hard to suppress surfaced with a quiver that was reflected in her voice as she replied, 'That's not a fair question, and you know it.'

His smile deepened teasingly. 'When did I ever play fair?'

Sheona could only be grateful when Jason broke the magic that was weaving itself about them by exclaiming enthusiastically, 'This beats a sun-ray lamp and a painted backdrop in a studio! I'd have done this job for *nothing* if I'd known.'

'Careful, Jason,' she cautioned, striving hard for normality. 'That's not the sort of thing you should say to the boss. He might just take you up on it.'

Marcus grinned and drove on, stopping in front of the house as a small coffee-coloured woman with iron-grey hair came out to greet them with an excited rush of words. She must have been all of sixty, possibly more, but her movements were quick and energetic and her lilting heavily accented English was interspersed with bursts of merry laughter.

She hugged Marcus, exclaimed over his explanation of Sheona not being Shireen, whom she knew, and hugged her anyway. Then she hugged Jason, whom she didn't know, for good measure.

'Louise, my housekeeper,' Marcus introduced as soon as he could get a word in edgeways. 'She's a law unto herself. When she doesn't feel like living here she disappears for days at a time. She's convinced our blood-lines meet somewhere, reputedly in my great-grandfather's time, and she trades on it mercilessly. I keep sacking her but she doesn't take a blind bit of notice.'

Louise giggled and ushered them all into the house. The rooms were large and airy, with big ceiling fans, and Indian bamboo furniture cohabited comfortably with western sofas and armchairs. Like the house in Richmond, this one had an air of homely comfort that took generations to achieve.

Louise took Jason in hand, and Marcus led Sheona up to her room. It was as spacious as the rooms below, with Indian rugs scattered over a gleaming, polished floor and a huge bed draped with a spotlessly white mosquito net. He showed her the switch that operated the overhead fan, telling her, 'We have our own generator so electricity's no problem, and the plumbing is modern.'

'It's a beautiful room,' she replied sincerely. 'I'd have loved it even without mod cons.'

Marcus gave her one of his piercing looks. 'You're very easy to please.'

Sheona smiled. 'If you call this easy you've got a different yardstick to measure everything by than I have.'

He turned away. 'You'll come out of this with enough to put the house in Bournemouth right.'

That hadn't been what Sheona had meant, but he was continuing, 'Your bathroom is through that door over there, and if you need any extra gear you'll find some of Shireen's clothes in the wardrobe.'

Sheona came down to earth with a thump. She'd been so entranced with the island and the house that she'd forgotten about Shireen. 'Marcus...?' she began impulsively.

He was about to leave her but he paused and looked back. 'Yes?'

She was on the point of asking whether his relationship with Shireen had been strictly business but, as an instant's reflection warned her, she couldn't. After all, there was no reason for her to care one way or the other—unless she cared for him. And that was the one thing he mustn't suspect.

'Nothing,' she replied awkwardly. 'I—er——' She stopped again, not knowing what to say.

Marcus looked at her frowningly, and came to his own conclusions. 'Shireen left some clothes because she expected to return to complete the commercials. She wasn't my mistress.'

Sheona's cheeks flooded with colour. 'That's not what I meant to ask.'

'Yes, it is. Ask me what you like, but don't lie to me. That's one thing I can't forgive.'

'We can't all be perfect,' she retorted, stung, but she was talking to thin air. Marcus had gone. Damn! Now he was mad at her again. It was a pity he didn't know what it was like to be so embarrassed that a white lie sprang to the lips purely as a matter of self-defence!

His curtness robbed her of all the joy she would have felt at discovering he and Shireen hadn't been lovers. All she could do now was wonder miserably whether he wished they had been.

Certainly something—something she hadn't got to the bottom of yet—was firing him up so that he lashed out at her at any and every opportunity.

Sheona tried to convince herself it was the unfairness of it all that made her feel so choked and upset as she wandered despondently to the open french windows. She went out on to the veranda and leaned on the rail, looking down over the green hills to the incredible turquoise of the ocean beyond. A sigh that seemed to come from her very soul escaped her.

Here she was, as close to paradise as she was ever likely to be, but it was a flawed paradise. It always would be, too, while the man she was obsessed with kept walking away from her as though he couldn't bear her company for long without losing all patience with her.

Those moments of closeness that she cherished must be purely imaginary, something she felt and he endured. That realisation gave a whole new meaning to the phrase 'a fool's paradise', and once again she vowed, 'No more!' This time she said it aloud, hoping that would help her to believe it.

Then she went back into her room, firmly closing the french windows behind her. She didn't know where Marcus's room was, but the veranda was a communal one and it was unnerving to think he could walk in on her any time he pleased.

She unpacked and changed into a bikini, pulling a matching mini-skirt and top over it that left her midriff bare. She slipped thonged beach shoes on to her feet, picked up a beach towel and slapped a wide straw hat she'd found in the wardrobe on her head. Shireen's, no doubt, but she wouldn't mind sharing it.

She walked straight into Marcus as she came out of her room. He was wearing shorts and a white T-shirt, his muscled arms and legs as brown as if he'd never left the island. He had a beach bag slung over his shoulder and his eyes flicked over her with the piercing intentness that was so peculiarly his own.

Sheona felt extraordinarily self-conscious, although the amount of flesh she was exposing was modest enough. Just as she was sure she couldn't fight down yet another blush much longer, he said, 'I see you've got a good all-over suntan already. That's very helpful. I thought you might only be tanned on your face.'

'It's been a good summer in England, and a long one,' she replied huskily, still unnerved by his close scrutiny. 'I've managed to get some sunbathing in on the patio at home, and sometimes on the beach. I live beside the sea, remember.'

'Are you wearing a good screening lotion?' he asked as they began to walk along the passage and down the stairs together.

'Well, no, I thought——'

'Whatever you thought, it isn't good enough,' he broke in. 'I'll make sure you're properly protected when we get to the beach. I thought you'd have more sense than to go out and boil yourself in the sun.'

'You don't have to fuss around me!' she flared, incensed.

'Until your sister arrives that's precisely what I have to do. You might be the "other twin", but you're the only one I've got at the moment.'

Nothing he'd said could have hurt her more. She suspected he knew it, too. Last night—this morning, even!— she'd been sure they'd been drawing closer. Now he was declaring war again, for reasons he naturally didn't think it necessary to explain to her.

How farcical that she could have imagined herself in love with this man! He was detestable! The problem was that only her head knew it. Her heart and her flesh still persisted in going their own wilful ways, as she was soon reminded when his shoulder accidentally brushed against her arm. Her nerve-endings couldn't have reacted more positively if she'd been burned.

'Sorry,' he apologised formally, stepping pointedly away from her.

'Not half as sorry as I am,' she retorted. Then, out on the veranda, she decided she couldn't face much more of this. She stopped short of the steps that led down to the garden, and said, 'This is silly. We clearly don't want to be with each other. Why don't I make it easy on us and go back to my room?'

'The object of bringing you out here early was to get you acclimatised and tanned the right colour before shooting starts,' he reminded her irritably. 'That will hardly be achieved if you sulk in your room.'

'I'm entitled to sulk, the way you treat me.'

Marcus caught her arm and swung her towards him. 'How exactly would you like me to treat you, Sheona?' he asked softly.

She wrenched herself away and stalked down the veranda steps, complaining bitterly, 'It would help if you stopped behaving as though this were all my fault. I'm fed up with being blamed for a situation that was none of my making.'

Marcus hesitated for a moment, then said quietly, 'Point taken.'

She supposed she could score that as a minor victory, but she was so uneasy with him as he led her through the garden that she asked, 'Where's Jason? Isn't he joining us?'

'No. He's taken one of the mokes to explore the island. We have several so the tourists can get about. They're not too keen on the bicycles and ox-carts used by the islanders.'

'It doesn't matter if Jason gets sunstroke, then!' she exclaimed bitterly. 'I don't see why I should be the only one to be supervised!'

'Jason's a professional model. I can depend on him to take very good care of himself,' he replied dismissively, and came to a halt as the land fell away to the sea.

'There's the granite I was telling you about,' he went on, and pointed to a mass of great black rocks that looked as though they'd been carved by a surrealist sculptor. 'There's a path through them to the beach. Do you think you can manage it? There's another track we could drive down, but this is more picturesque.'

Sheona was enchanted against her will, and she admitted, 'I'd much rather walk.'

'That's my girl,' he replied, not for the first time, and she wished more fervently than ever that he'd stop saying that. She was *not* his girl!

Marcus seemed totally unaware of the turmoil her emotions were in as he went first down the path, giving her an excellent opportunity to study his lithe body as she followed. It didn't do her blood-pressure any good, nor her temper when she found she was watching him more than where she was going.

Her feet slipped a little in her sandals, adding to her difficulty, so she stopped and took them off.

'Are you all right?' he asked.

'Fine,' she retorted, distrusting his concern. If he weren't so obsessed with his commercials she was sure it wouldn't bother him too much if she broke her neck.

He did pause to offer her his hand at a particularly steep bit, but she brushed it aside, saying proudly, 'I can manage.'

He didn't offer her any more help, and she was just as incensed about that. There's no pleasing me, she admitted to herself in a moment of self-honesty, knowing that whatever he did or said now she would react in a hostile manner. She didn't blame herself for that, though. It was Marcus's own ambivalent attitude to her that was colouring her reactions to him.

Talk about blowing hot and cold—without forgetting the great chunks of indifference in between!

Sheona found she had plenty of bitter things to remember to bolster up her hostility, and she remembered all of them as she glowered resentfully at Marcus's broad shoulders and slim hips on the rest of the descent through the granite rocks.

By the time they reached the beach she was in such a state of rebellion that she was unprepared to be pleased with anything about him or his island. She felt she could fight them both on any level, at any time, then one look around robbed her of all her antagonism and resentment, and her lips parted in an involuntary gasp of wonder.

Her feet were sinking sensuously into the warm white sand of a beach shaped into a perfect crescent as it stretched towards the gently rhythmic waves of a turquoise ocean. At either end smooth black granite rocks marked its boundaries, and in between was a profusion of graceful palm trees. The only man-made intrusion was a beach sunshade, thatched so that it looked entirely natural.

Marcus was watching her face. She was aware of that, but she couldn't keep the wonder out of her eyes as she exclaimed, 'Is this real? Is it honestly real? Oh, Marcus, I didn't think anything could be so perfect this side of heaven!'

She thought a kind of wonder filled his own eyes as they met hers. He took a hasty step towards her but then he stopped, as though pulled back against his will. After an infinitesimal moment in which he appeared to be struggling with himself, he replied impersonally, 'Now you know why I'm filming the commercials here. If this location can't sell the perfume, what can?'

His practicality was like a douche of cold water to Sheona. She recoiled and said scornfully, 'Of course! The video you showed me was filmed here, wasn't it? I suppose the next two will involve the path through the granite and the house?'

'You suppose right,' he replied coolly.

'So your commercial instincts don't stop at debasing your own home!' she exclaimed contemptuously, her artistic soul offended.

'If it weren't for my commercial instincts this wouldn't still be my home,' he retorted. 'The time has long gone when a cinnamon plantation could support all this. We pay our workers, you know—they're not slaves. For years my family survived on invested capital but there wasn't much left by the time I inherited. It was a case of supporting the island by other means, making it pay for itself, or selling. I took the first two options.'

Marcus paused to let that sink in, then added, 'These commercials, if they're successful, will create extra security for the island by establishing another successful business. The publicity for the perfume will also be publicity for the island, attracting more tourists, which was a major factor in deciding to film here. I don't call that debasing the island, but helping to preserve it along with the lifestyle of its people.'

Sheona felt a rush of shame at where her hostility had led her. She had rushed in, making unjustifiable snap judgements, and all because she didn't want to see, hear or believe anything good about Marcus.

'I'm sorry,' she apologised, biting her lip in chagrin. 'I spoke out of turn. I—I—wasn't thinking. In fact, if all this were mine I'd put on a hula-hula skirt and dance for the tourists if that would help!'

'I can't see myself in a hula-hula skirt, but I'll bear it in mind,' Marcus murmured, straight-faced.

Sheona giggled, tried to stop, then giggled again. 'You know what I mean,' she protested with laughing indignation.

'I know how you sound when you're amused, and I like it,' he replied huskily.

Her heart began to thump painfully against her ribs, unable to cope with the emotion that surged through it as her eyes bathed in the warmth of his. It was another timeless moment when the antipathy between them had no reality, no meaning.

Warning bells rang in her head, but she didn't want to listen to warning bells. She wanted...she wanted...Marcus!

She turned away from him, she had to, afraid of what he would read in her eyes—but he was already turning away, a fraction ahead of her in his rejection. She didn't know why, but it was hurtful and humiliating, and she despaired at how vulnerable just one unguarded glance could make her.

Her body chemistry, all her feelings, seemed to be trying to burn a lifetime of living into days, hours, as if they knew she would never again experience the raw and all-consuming emotions Marcus aroused in her.

She was ashamed to think how she would have gloried in all she was feeling if Marcus had given her more than just the fleeting moments of encouragement he specialised in, encouragement that was almost immediately withdrawn.

She suspected he was deliberately winding her up, so that, if it came to a camera session, her emotions would already be simmering on the surface, easy to stir to get the effect he wanted.

It was a horrible thought, but one she couldn't easily dismiss. She knew, she just *knew* that sometimes he shared the emotions that were shattering her, so why did he suppress them so forcefully—unless for a very good reason?

She could only think of two: the cameras...or Shireen. Either—or both—was obviously more important to him than unleashing the passion that alternately bound them together and tore them apart.

No wonder she despaired! She didn't want to be some kind of passionate plaything, but neither did she want to be rejected in such a callous way.

Sheona looked beautiful and vibrant as she followed Marcus along the beach, but inside she felt small and insignificant—truly the 'other twin' again, with a vengeance!

He led her to the shade of the thatched beach umbrella, opening his beach bag and taking out a towel. Sheona spread hers in the sunshine, stripped to her bikini and sat down. She kept her back towards him and looked moodily out to sea.

The next thing she knew his hand was on her shoulder, and she jumped, recoiling from his touch as though she'd been scorched.

'For heaven's sake, I haven't brought you down here to rape you,' Marcus said irritably. 'It's only the screening lotion to block out the harmful rays of the sun.'

'Oh.' She felt more than a little foolish at her violent reaction, but he wasn't to know the wild sensations any contact with him aroused in her.

She was keyed up to fever pitch as he massaged the lotion across her shoulders. She couldn't remember ever experiencing anything quite so provocatively sensual as the deliberate way his hand moved over her sensitive skin.

Deliberate? It was almost—almost—loving, but she'd been down that blind alley with him before. It was a terrible struggle, though, to stop herself relaxing, softening, as he moved the slender strings of her bikini to massage underneath, then worked his way down to her lower back. Just as she felt she could endure no more without whimpering for mercy, he said, 'Lie down.'

She lay on her stomach and the exquisite torture began again from the top of her legs to the soles of her feet, and when it finally stopped she was, perversely, sorry.

'I suppose you'd prefer to do the front yourself,' he said.

'Of course I would,' she said with a frigidity she was far from feeling as she sat up and took the lotion from him.

'Then make a thorough job of it.'

He watched her closely as she smoothed lotion over every remaining inch of her exposed skin. 'The mole is very—provocative,' he said.

'Mole? What mole?' she asked, taken by surprise.

'The one you don't share with Shireen.'

Sheona looked down at her upper thigh and the tiny mole that was only exposed when she wore the briefest of bikinis. The thought of him studying her there made her blush.

'Blushing is very provocative, too,' he murmured.

Before she could reply he turned and sat with his back towards her. 'My turn,' he said, nodding to the lotion.

He was already very brown and she found herself biting her lip as she began to give him some of his own treatment, her hands discovering a skill she didn't know they possessed as she massaged the lotion over his muscled shoulders and back.

How intimate this was, how incredibly seductive...

'That's it,' she snapped, passing the lotion over his shoulder to him, and promptly lying face-down on her towel. Closing her eyes wasn't much of a way of isolating herself from him, but it was the only option she had.

'Fifteen minutes either side as your skin's already seasoned,' he said. 'You can have another short sunning session late this afternoon if you feel comfortable, but cover up in between to be on the safe side. No sense in taking chances.'

No sense at all, she thought, but it wasn't her suntan she was worried about as he lay down beside her. She thought of surreptitiously inching herself away from him but there was a vicarious thrill in having him so close to her.

It was a thrill that overrode caution. A thrill she couldn't resist.

CHAPTER NINE

SADLY, it wasn't a thrill Marcus seemed to share. Sheona was so acutely conscious of him that she sensed his restlessness long before he thrust himself to his feet and said, 'I'm going for a swim.'

He didn't invite her to join him.

She turned over on her back and looked up at the sky, a limitless blue with not a puff of a cloud anywhere. Idyllic, but not for her. Now that Marcus was gone she felt restless herself. Bored, but she was always bored when he wasn't with her. Well, not bored precisely, but not happy. She was in limbo—a state of waiting. Waiting for him to come back.

She hated herself for it.

Better to lie here looking at the sky than to search the sea for him, she thought, but the second after she came to that conclusion she was sitting up, searching.

She saw him almost immediately. There was no reef to create a tame lagoon and he was powering out to sea with a relaxed and tireless overarm stroke. She allowed herself the luxury of watching him for a few minutes, then she felt even more cut off from him, even more miserable.

She stood up and wandered along the beach, searching for shells as though such a childish pastime still held charm for her. It might have done, too, if she hadn't been so obsessed with Marcus. But she was fidgety, edgy, and soon the heat of the sun, or her longing for him, drove her into the sea as well.

She was a powerful swimmer herself, but she played rather than swam, diving to look at the spotless seabed and the exotic fish that seemed to accept her as one of their own. She felt as close to being a mermaid as it was possible to feel and she would have been completely happy—if only it hadn't been for Marcus.

She dived and dived again, losing all consciousness of time in her effort to lose all consciousness of the man who so obsessed her. She was always on a non-starter, though, and she eventually gave up. She surfaced from what she meant to be the last dive, her long hair streaming across her face.

Sheona smoothed it back with both hands as she trod water, blinking in the sunlight. Through her fingers she saw Marcus, so close that he must have been waiting for her to come up.

Had he been watching her twist and turn and glide with the fish, completely free from the self-consciousness that inhibited her so dreadfully when she was with him?

'You look as if you're in your natural element,' he said, treading water with her. Sunlight glinted on drops of crystal-clear water falling from his arm as he lifted it from the sea to push back from her face a strand of hair that she'd missed.

It seemed almost a possessive gesture, and it did terrible things to her heartbeat. There was no mistaking, either, that his voice was warm with approval. Sheona instantly felt self-conscious again, but the feeling of completeness that overcame her whenever he was close meant that she couldn't harden herself against him, reject his friendliness.

'Funny you should say that—I was just thinking how wonderful it would be to be a mermaid,' she replied, smiling with a brilliance she could never manage for the cameras.

'I was thinking you looked like one, but I'm glad you're not.'

'Why?' she asked innocently.

'Because then you'd be lost to the human race—lost to me.'

Sheona didn't know what he meant, and she was so afraid of misinterpreting him that she dived again. 'Lost to me.' Surely he could only be referring to his need to get his wretched commercials finished? she thought as she made her escape down to the seabed.

She was startled to find he'd dived, too, and was even more startled when he caught her hand and swam with her. Then a feeling of irresponsibility overcame her and she stopped fighting whatever force it was that drew them together. He was smiling, and she smiled back, surrendering to the enjoyment of the moment.

This time it was the two of them who twisted and turned and played among the fish, except that they seemed to move as one. There was nothing antagonistic between them now, only complete harmony. Sheona felt divorced from the real world above, and all her problems dissolved to nothing. She was momentarily completely and blissfully happy.

Marcus seemed to know when she needed air and powered his way to the surface, pulling her up after him. They smiled at each other in the sunlight, then dived and played again.

His hand kept a firm clasp on hers and Sheona could have played all afternoon, but after one of their surfacings he said, 'We must do this again some time,' and she knew that it was over.

They swam slowly back to the beach, Marcus adjusting his stroke to hers. It added to her feeing of completeness, to the certainty that—just for a little while—they had been thinking, feeling and behaving as one.

They became two people again as they walked out of the sea on to the beach, picking up their towels and drying themselves. Sheona could actually feel the separation happening, and it wasn't at her will, it was at his.

The world had returned to Marcus. She was still resisting.

It came back to her too, though, when he said, 'You're one up on Shireen when it comes to swimming. She prefers to look at the sea from the beach.'

Shireen again!

He had played with her, Sheona, and promptly thought of her sister. She was still a substitute, then, still the 'other twin'.

'Shireen swims well enough,' she replied, the edge on her voice cutting through the last of their lingering harmony. 'It's just that a model on an assignment has to consider her appearance all the time. She can't keep washing sea salt out of her hair, can she?'

Marcus put his hand under her chin and lifted her face to his. 'You're very loyal,' he murmured.

'So is Shireen.'

His face twisted and he let her go. 'To you, maybe. Her friends aren't so fortunate.'

'If you think that then you don't really know Shireen,' she retorted.

'Or you don't,' he replied.

Sheona snatched up her clothes and said, 'If you'd turn round I'd like to get changed.'

He turned without another word and she had the dubious pleasure of watching his back as she modestly took off her bikini and put on her mini-skirt and top. He had no such inhibitions, stripping off his bathers so that she had a brief glimpse of his muscled, suntanned buttocks before he pulled on his shorts.

She envied him his ability to be so natural but it only proved, she thought dejectedly, just how unconscious he was of her when it suited him. Which was most of the time.

She was subdued as they climbed the path between the granite boulders, and she was puffing slightly as she reached the top. Marcus was waiting for her, breathing easily, and he said with a slight smile, 'My mermaid not so happy on dry land?'

Sheona resented the 'my' so much that she allowed her misery to show by retorting unguardedly, 'Happy? What's happy?'

The next thing she knew she was in his arms, her soft breasts crushed against the hardness of his chest. Her mouth opened in a gasp before it, too, was crushed under the fierce demand of his lips. She was shocked and unprepared, but her body wasn't. All the yearning trapped within her exploded in an exultant joy that increased with every wild and wilful beat of her singing heart.

She felt they were one again, with nothing to be hidden or denied between them, and a joy that was purer than the earthy needs of her body brought the moistness of tears to her eyes. She was surrendering, and so was he. She was sure of it.

Marcus's breath was coming as raggedly as hers when he finally raised his head, breaking the exquisite union of their lips as he stared down at her with a blazing wildness she understood and shared.

Then, disbelievingly, she saw the wildness fade as though he was deliberately smothering it along with everything that existed—or might have existed—between them.

'Now you know what happy is,' he said harshly.

Before she could recover, or even pretend to recover, he thrust her from him and strode away.

* * *

Sheona retreated into a world of her own. She looked the same, she seemed the same, but she knew she never would be the same. Marcus had rejected her once too often. She simply couldn't absorb any more of the emotional shocks he kept inflicting on her.

They met again at lunch, when they both behaved as though nothing had happened between them. For Marcus, perhaps, nothing much had—but that was the measure of the difference between them.

Jason joined them for the light meal of cold meats, salad and fruit, and he chattered away about his exploration of the island. 'It's like one huge aviary,' he said enthusiastically. 'It's weird seeing so many parrots and things flying free. I mean, I've never seen anything like it outside of a zoo before.'

'Try some diving,' Sheona recommended, determined to shoulder her share of the conversation for fear Marcus would think she was sulking—or, even worse, hurt!—if she stayed silent. 'It's like one huge fish tank. I swam among tropical fish this morning that I never even knew existed.'

'These islands only started to be settled two hundred years ago, so the bird- and plant-life have had millions of years to evolve undisturbed,' Marcus explained. 'That's why so much of it is unique. There are some books in the sitting-room that will tell you more, if you're interested.'

'I'm not much of a one for books,' Jason admitted frankly. 'I'd rather ask you about things I want to know.'

'Fair enough,' Marcus replied easily, then his dark eyes settled on Sheona. 'And you?' he asked.

'I'll look at the books if there's time.'

'What do you mean, "if there's time"?' Jason asked. 'There'll be heaps of time.'

'Not for me. The minute Shireen gets here I'm returning to England.'

'Gosh, that doesn't seem fair.' Jason looked at Marcus. 'Does she have to go?'

'No, she doesn't,' he replied. 'Sheona can stay on for a holiday if she wishes.'

'I don't wish,' she interjected waspishly. 'I have my own career to get on with.'

'Surely your career is not as important as being out here?' Jason asked, sunnily unaware of the tension crackling in the air around him.

'Not to anybody but me, obviously,' she replied, her honeyed malice aimed directly at Marcus.

He knew it, too. He gave her one of his enigmatic looks, but it was left to Jason to say, 'Well, I think it's a shame.'

'Believe me, Jason, it will be a blessed release. I love these islands but I loathe anything to do with modelling. To be allowed to escape from it all—that's what I call happy.'

It was another gibe at Marcus, and this time he responded, 'That's not what I call happy, it's what I call evading the issue.'

'What issue?' Jason asked, bewildered, but Marcus was already rising from his chair.

'You'll have to excuse me now,' he said, as though he'd lost interest in the conversation, even though Sheona was glowering at him. 'I have some campaign layouts that have to be airmailed back to London as soon as I've approved them. I want to get them on the launch when it calls in this afternoon. If either of you is going out for any length of time ask Louise for a drink you can take with you. If you get thirsty you won't find a café on every corner the way you would at an English resort.'

He went out. Sheona's heart might have felt as heavy as stone but she couldn't prevent her eyes from watching him go. Such was the impact of his physical presence that she still felt it even after the door had closed behind him.

It hurt so much, the many different ways he had of shutting her out.

Jason, sinking his white teeth into a piece of fresh coconut, dragged her out of her reverie by asking, 'What are you going to do this afternoon?'

Try to forget about this morning, she thought, but aloud she said, 'Find somewhere shady and do some sketching.'

'Of course, you're some sort of an artist, aren't you?'

'Some sort,' she agreed wryly.

'Sure you wouldn't rather come diving with me?' he persisted, as oblivious to irony as ever. 'I mean to get a look at those fish you were talking about.'

'No, thanks,' she replied. She would be reminded of Marcus too much, and Jason, inoffensive as he was, was just no substitute for the man who obsessed her from the moment her eyes opened in the morning until they closed at night—and often during the long and lonely hours in between.

Whichever way she looked at it, she would be much better off on her own this afternoon. In fact, she craved solitude as she had never craved it before. She lingered at the table only long enough to allow Jason to get well clear, then she, too, made her excuses and left.

She'd thrown a sketchbook, a bundle of pencils and a box of colouring sticks in her suitcase simply because she was as incapable of travelling without them as her toothbrush and paste. She retrieved them from her room, along with her glasses and straw hat, and wandered down into the garden.

She went round to the back of the house and found it was almost identical to the front, although this was obviously an area to relax in. The tropical vegetation had been cut back to make a lawn, and scattered about it were wicker chairs and tables under huge parasols. There were also sun-loungers, and even hammocks slung between the trees bordering the grass.

Sheona glanced at the open french windows of the house and wondered which room Marcus was working in. Whatever, he was too close for comfort and she wandered on along a path that wound lazily around trees and flowering bushes.

She picked examples of leaves and flowers she wanted to draw as she went, thinking what an exotic addition they would make to her portfolio, which her clients liked to look through for ideas when they commissioned a specific piece.

What was Marcus doing now—still working?

The question shot unwanted into her brain, making her groan in despair and plunge along a path that branched off from the main one, as though losing herself would also help her to lose her tortured thoughts of him.

Except that there was no chance of losing herself on this particular path. It opened abruptly on nothing but the sea. She sat under the shade of a tree, took off her hat and stuck the stems of the specimens she'd picked through the straw of the crown, turning it into a make-shift display area. She rested the hat on a rock, turned the specimens to the angle she wanted, put on her glasses and began to draw.

She didn't know how much time passed and she didn't care. By absorbing herself in her work she was able to reduce the ache that was Marcus to an almost bearable level. She sketched every specimen from several angles, sometimes with fine pencil work, sometimes with bold splashes of colour, until she felt she could recreate them with vivid accuracy long after Drummond Island was no more than a bitter-sweet memory.

More bitter than sweet, she thought sadly, but she was terribly afraid it was the sweetest of those rare moments when Marcus was nice to her that she would remember most.

She hoped the Indian summer was still holding in England, so that her return wouldn't be too much of a shock. Then she wondered whether it would be easy to pick up the threads of her real life, or whether they would be as frayed and broken as she felt they were now.

She sighed. Her concentration was going. Marcus was crowding in on her once more, robbing her of what little peace she'd managed to find, demanding her whole heart and mind and attention. She sighed again, and this time there was weariness mingled with her misery. Her effort to block him out had robbed her of all her creative and nervous energy, leaving her drained and exhausted.

Sheona took off her glasses and picked up her hat, sorrowfully removing the wilting specimens from the crown and throwing them away. If only love—or infatuation, or whatever it was she felt for Marcus!—would wilt as quickly as these exotic blooms when it was parted from its life force. No such luck, though. It just seemed to generate its own power, a power that increased with or without encouragement.

She found herself sinking down on the soft earth, closing her eyes, seeking the oblivion that sleep might bring. Hopefully...

She dreamed of him, but her dream was a delight, not a torment. Marcus was smiling at her, his eyes warm and tender, his touch gentle as he reached down carefully to smooth away a wayward strand of hair from her face.

Then he lifted her head and shoulders from the ground and cradled her in his arms, holding her so lovingly that her heart almost burst with happiness. He was so real that in her dream she quivered. 'Marcus,' she murmured. 'Marcus...'

'Ssh, go back to sleep. You're quite safe.' He put her down carefully and went away, taking the dream with him.

Sighing, she slept on.

She awoke an hour or so later, the euphoria of her dream still clinging to her, and even the sadness of knowing it had all been make-believe didn't quite shatter the peace that had come to her. She moved slowly and languorously, as though Marcus really had cradled her in his arms. She was sorrowfully reluctant to lose the image and the feeling of him watching over her while she slept.

Finally, though, discomforts other than her longing for him forced her to sit up. She was dreadfully thirsty, and she'd been so deep in thought when she'd left the house that she'd forgotten to ask Louise for a drink. On top of that, moving made her aware that her head was aching slightly. As if that wasn't enough, the earth that had seemed so soft when she'd sunk down exhausted now felt hard and unkind to her softer body.

She gathered her glasses and sketching materials together and stood up, looking around to make sure she'd left nothing behind. It was then that she saw the folded-up shirt where her head had rested, and a vacuum flask beside it.

She stared and stared, unable to believe what she was seeing. Then she reached down and shook out the shirt, recognising it instantly as the one Marcus had worn at lunch. So he had been here! But the rest of it—surely the rest of it had been the pure imaginary longing of a feverish dream?

It couldn't really have happened, not the way she remembered it. Marcus cradling her lovingly like that, as though he really cared. No, of course not! And yet he'd been thoughtful enough to put his shirt under her head to protect her from the rough earth.

Not protecting *me*, she told herself fiercely—protecting his model.

And yet the thought of him touching her, lifting her while she'd been utterly defenceless, made her quiver more violently than she had in her dream, and blush fierily for good measure.

Oh, if only she knew how much of it had been real, and how much merely grafted on by her dream! The flask was real enough, that was for sure, and her fingers weren't quite steady as she reached down for it. She took the cup from the top, unscrewed the cap and poured the clear liquid from the flask to the cup. She tasted it cautiously, then drank deeply. It was pure lemonade, chilled and slightly under-sweetened, just the way she liked it.

She drank a second cupful, then a third, and her headache eased. She realised she must have been dehydrating. Whatever she felt about Marcus, she was very grateful to him for leaving the flask. She would have to thank him, and that would be embarrassing. No, it wouldn't, she corrected herself quickly. He might possess the most uncanny perception where she was concerned, but even he couldn't guess what went on in her dreams.

Could he?

On that uncertain note Sheona began the return trip to the house, occupying herself by rehearsing a polite little speech of thanks for the lemonade and the pillow he'd made of his shirt. She only hoped she didn't give herself away by blushing self-consciously before she was halfway through it.

In a way she was let off the hook because when she reached the garden both Marcus and Jason were lazing on sun-loungers, and she never felt quite as awkward with Marcus when somebody else was about.

When he opened his eyes and stared at her with his own particular brand of intensity, though, she forgot every line of her rehearsed speech. 'Your shirt and your flask,' she said, putting them both down on the wicker table beside him. 'I don't know how you found me, but both were much appreciated, thank you.'

'Louise saw which way you went, and she told me you hadn't dropped by the kitchen for refreshments, so I thought I'd better do my boy-scout act,' he replied casually.

Boy-scout act...so that was the way he looked at it. That meant the dream of him cradling her lovingly in his arms had never been more than a dream. Well, she'd always known that, hadn't she? 'I won't be so forgetful next time,' she replied, trying to match his casualness.

'Next time I'll be with you. I don't feel easy about you wandering off by yourself until you're properly acclimatised.'

'I'm not a child,' she retorted.

'No,' he agreed drily, his dark eyes roving over her in a suggestive way that filled her with a pulsing, forbidden excitement, 'you're definitely not a child. You just behave like one sometimes, that's all.'

'I do not!'

'Sound like one, then, like right now,' he corrected easily.

Jason raised his head and looked at them. 'Are you two quarrelling?' he asked.

'No,' Marcus replied. 'Sheona is just going to change into her bikini to join us for her second sunning of the day.'

It was a command and she knew it. She went towards the house with a decided flounce, and when she came out again she had a beach robe over her bikini. She took it off as she settled herself pointedly on the lounger furthest away from Marcus.

The next thing she knew he was standing over her, smiling and murmuring, 'Definitely not a child, but still with a lot of growing up to do for all that.'

She glowered at him, but then he was massaging the screening lotion over her back again, his knowing hands subjecting her once more to the most exquisite torture. She didn't know whether she was glad or sorry when Jason splintered the tension that was inexorably building up between them by asking, 'I could do with some more lotion when you're finished.'

Silently Marcus handed it to Sheona, and when she'd finished smoothing it over her front he took it over to Jason. She lay down, her body still glowing with the touch of Marcus's hands, wanting more, and not so very far from demanding more.

Oh, help! Wherever Shireen was, Sheona prayed she would shift herself to Drummond Island without any further loss of time. She really couldn't endure much more of this. It was like—like—dicing with seduction, and the fact that Jason was there as a kind of unwitting chaperon didn't seem to make a whole lot of difference.

Was this really her, quiet and responsible Sheona Murray, thinking and feeling these wild and irresponsible things? It didn't seem possible...

She spent twenty minutes pretending to look the picture of relaxation, when all the time the effort of keeping her eyes away from Marcus was crisping her nerves to a frazzle. Then Jason created a small diversion by going back into the house, and she had to endure another ten minutes of pretence before Marcus more or less marched her back, too.

'That's enough exposure for today,' he told her. 'You're tanning beautifully. A couple more sessions and you'll be as close to Shireen's colour in the first commercial as makes no difference.'

Just the mention of the commercials made her jumpier than ever. Without any hope she asked, 'Have you heard from her?'

'No.'

Did he hesitate fractionally before he replied? For a moment Sheona thought that he did, then she told herself she was imagining things. Marcus had no reason to lie to her. Besides, he needed her twin even more than she did, and once he knew where Shireen was he'd be off to drag her here himself if necessary.

All the same, she felt a twinge of unease that persisted until Marcus sidetracked her by saying, 'Dinner will be in a couple of hours. Louise isn't exactly an on-the-dot person but it will be served somewhere around eight.'

He stopped at the bottom of the stairs, leaning on the banister and smiling as he added, 'Don't wait until eight. Come down whenever you're ready for pre-dinner drinks on the veranda—what we call sundowners out here.'

And it seemed to her that his smile was exactly the same as it had been in her dream—gentle, loving, tender.

Sheona walked up the stairs in a daze. She had to get away from this little scrap of paradise called Drummond Island before it was too late. It was having the weirdest effect on her, merging dreams and reality, reality and dreams, until she could no longer tell them apart.

Or didn't want to.

CHAPTER TEN

SHEONA bathed and changed into an ankle-length gown of coral chiffon. It suited her dark colouring, enhanced her tan, and its loose draping across her bosom and floating layers of skirt were flatteringly feminine. It was a man-trap, and she didn't dare to look too closely into her reasons for wearing it.

She only knew that tonight she wanted to look her best, and that she had succeeded. Her long hair fell glossily down her back, her lips were coloured coral to match her gown and her large brown eyes were dramatised with smoky shadow and mascara.

She had never looked, nor felt as intensely feminine as she did now. Deep down inside she knew that she had dressed with such care for Marcus's benefit, and Marcus's alone.

Marcus... the man who'd rejected her so often and so painfully, the man she'd sworn would never get the chance to hurt her again. And yet all this effort was prompted by him. It was perverse, but so was her infatuation for him.

The truth was that she had no control over her behaviour. It was too instinctive. Tonight, whatever happened, Marcus would be made aware of all he had so determinedly rejected.

It all came down to pride, she supposed with a cynicism alien to her character. Pride... the ultimate refuge of a woman scorned!

She twisted and turned before the mirror, looking critically for faults and finding none. She was as ready as she was ever going to be. She walked out on to the veranda, killing time. She must give Marcus time to miss her—if he was capable of missing her.

She heard the murmur of men's voices on the veranda below and her heart missed a beat as she distinguished Marcus's deeper tone from Jason's. To distract herself she stared out at the ocean, transformed to crimson and gold by the setting sun. She was stunned by the beauty of it all, and felt forlorn that Marcus wasn't with her to share it.

So much life, so much awareness was pulsing within her this evening that she scarcely knew what to do with herself. It must be the magic of the tropics, she told herself. The magic of Marcus, an inner voice corrected, and she ached almost unbearably to be with him.

'Sheona.'

His voice was so soft that at first she thought it was nothing but the sea breeze giving voice to her yearning for him. Then she felt his touch on her shoulder, so light that it scarcely pressed the filmy chiffon against her flesh.

She didn't quiver or flinch away from him. She accepted his presence—his touch—as though she'd known he would come to her. Well, not known, perhaps. Nothing about Marcus could ever be *known*. But hoped...

'I did knock,' he went on softly. 'You didn't hear me out here.'

She half turned towards him but she couldn't bring herself to look at his face, so afraid was she that his uncanny perceptiveness would pick up all she was feeling at this moment. He was wearing a lightweight white suit, and looking so incredibly handsome that her silk-clad legs almost buckled.

'I was fascinated by the sunset,' she replied, hoping he didn't notice the little catch in her voice, or suspect how hard it was to stop her body swaying towards his.

'I don't think I've ever seen anything so beautiful in my whole life.'

'Neither have I,' he replied huskily, ignoring the sunset and looking at her.

Wonderingly she raised her eyes to his. She wanted so much to believe what she read in them but she couldn't, her fear of yet another rejection stifling her hopes. 'You don't have to hype me up tonight,' she told him breathlessly. 'The cameras aren't due to roll until Wednesday, are they?'

'Damn the cameras,' he said roughly, but she had splintered the almost claustrophobic atmosphere between them, brought cold sanity into the madness of the moment. He removed his hand from her shoulder and stepped back a pace. 'I brought you this,' he said. 'It's time you used it. I happen to think that believing in a product helps to sell it.'

He placed in her hand a cut-glass bottle with a wooden top deliberately carved to look rough and primitive. She read the legend 'Slave' emblazoned on the label and her lips curved into a bitter smile. A desperate boldness she didn't know she was capable of made her say, 'If you believe your own publicity won't my using this make you—vulnerable?'

'I'll take my chances,' he replied, the old curtness returning to his voice.

'Well, I won't,' she replied, placing the bottle on the veranda rail and leaving it there. 'I'll wait until I meet a man I wouldn't mind enslaving.'

It was a colossal snub, of course, but it was only a fraction of what she owed him. The problem was that, in getting her own back, she seemed to hurt herself far more than she hurt him.

They didn't seem to have anything more to say to each other after that, and by tacit consent they left the sunset, the veranda, and the privacy of her room for the safety of Jason's company downstairs. Unasked, Marcus mixed a spritzer heavily loaded with ice and gave it to her, saying, 'Unless you'd like something stronger?'

'No, thanks,' she responded with the airy confidence that Jason's presence gave her. 'I'm the twin who believes in moderation in all things, not that Shireen's much different in that respect.'

'I thought I'd made it perfectly plain that I never, ever forget which twin I'm with,' Marcus replied, the steely edge on his voice cutting through her confidence like a knife. She felt again the familiar trepidation that his disapproval always aroused in her, and she jumped nervously as he put his own glass down on a table with a decided click.

Marcus frowned at her, biting back something he obviously wanted to say, and turned away. 'I'll see what's holding up dinner,' he went on, and left as though he couldn't bear her company for a moment longer, even with Jason there.

Sheona was left to ponder miserably on where her defiance had led her, and she felt so low that she didn't even hear what Jason was talking about. 'Sheona,' he repeated patiently, 'for the second time, what's the matter between you and Marcus? You always seem to be on the verge of a quarrel and I never know what it's about. What am I missing?'

She stared at him, but it took her a few seconds to bring him into focus, so wrapped up was she in Marcus's stormy eyes and even stormier departure. 'Nothing,' she managed at last.

'Look, I may not be Mensa material but I know when something's wrong,' Jason persisted. 'It's nothing to do with me, is it?'

'No, of course not. It's just that Marcus and I are—are—well, sort of chalk and cheese.'

'You mean you don't fancy each other?'

She almost laughed in bitter irony, but instead she lied, 'You've got it.'

'I don't suppose you happen to fancy me, then?' he asked. 'I'm missing my girlfriend.'

Sheona would have been affronted had he been anybody but Jason, but he was so patently guileless that she smiled and said gently, 'No, I'm afraid I don't.'

'I didn't think you did,' he agreed. 'I hope you didn't mind my asking.'

'I'm sure she didn't,' Marcus replied coldly from the french window, making Sheona jump and wonder how much of the conversation he'd overheard. Not that it mattered, but why the ice in his tone? He had no reason to be protective towards her.

'It's a pity, though,' Jason went on to Sheona, as though Marcus's disapproval hadn't registered at all. 'If we had something going between us it would make the commercials really sizzle, wouldn't it?'

'That's what you're being paid to simulate. It doesn't have to be real,' Marcus snapped.

Jason looked so hurt that Sheona felt obliged to intervene, 'I still don't think I'll actually be in the commercials. Shireen's bound to be here in time to let me off the hook.'

'The hook?' Marcus repeated, icier than ever.

'What would you call it, then?' she demanded, suddenly fed up with keeping the peace—fed up with everything!

'There you two go again,' Jason complained plaintively. 'Quarrelling without telling me what it's all about.'

'It's the way we are,' Marcus replied shortly. 'You'll get used to it.'

Which is more than I will, Sheona thought, all her old resentment flaring to the surface. This beautiful evening, this beautiful gown she was wearing, the trouble she'd taken with her appearance—all were wasted on a man who had about as much sensitivity as a stone. Why, oh, why did she keep trying so hard? Especially when she hated herself for trying at all?

The setting sun lit all their faces with glowing colour, making both men seem incredibly handsome. Suddenly Sheona thought she understood why she was over-reacting to everything in a way that would be inconceivable in England.

It was the tropics, exaggerating everything, heating her blood, exciting her senses, making a mockery of the calm good sense that normally characterised her.

Was this what had happened to Shireen?

It no longer seemed quite so preposterous that Shireen could have stolen Annabelle Drummond's boyfriend and run away with him, abandoning everything she'd held most dear in the delirium of the moment. Sheona could almost visualise herself doing the same thing if Marcus gave her the right encouragement.

Almost? She knew damn well that she would!

A gong sounded somewhere in the house and Marcus took her arm. 'Dinner,' he said, leading her into the dining-room while Jason followed amiably behind. 'The food in the Seychelles reflects the nationalities of the people who settled these islands—English, French, Indian and Chinese among them—but tonight we're having local Creole dishes. I hope you like your food spicy.'

'I do,' Sheona replied, unable to think of anything but the touch of his fingers on her bare arm. His mood seemed to be changing. Softening...

Bowls of exotic flowers provided vivid splashes of colour on the large and gleaming mahogany table. Marcus, seeing her look at them, smiled as he seated her and said, 'It's claimed that everything blooms twice out here. It certainly seems like it.'

This, she thought as a maid began to serve the first course, was definitely a different Marcus. Smiling, courteous, keeping the conversation going effortlessly—the perfect host. No trace of any antipathy towards her. In fact, as the meal progressed he made her feel as if he really wanted her there beside him.

It was impossible not to feel valued, pampered, and she would have had to be made of iron to resist the atmosphere he was creating. Being made very much of vulnerable flesh, she began to soften herself. Almost without realising it, she relaxed until she was enjoying Marcus's company as much as when they'd been diving together. She even felt she didn't need Jason's presence to make her feel secure, so powerful was the charm that Marcus was exerting over her.

She drank a glass of wine with the melon that was served as a starter, and smilingly allowed Marcus to refill her glass as they began the saffron-flavoured chicken served with Riz Creole, a rice dish cooked with ginger, onions and garlic.

The last brilliant glow of the sunset faded from the room and, at a nod from Marcus, the maid lit the candles in the silver candelabra on the table, and Sheona thought that perhaps it was a good thing that she had Jason as a chaperon, after all. This was heady stuff.

Dreamily she imagined generations of Drummond men dining romantically by candlelight with their women, just as she was now. Then she wished she was less imaginative as a pang of regret seared through her. She wasn't a Drummond woman, and never likely to be.

'Something wrong, Sheona?' Marcus asked, his quick concern taking her hurt away. Hard to believe now that this was the same man whose insensitivity frequently drove her up the wall.

'No, nothing,' she denied with a smile. 'I was just thinking how timeless all this seems.'

'Then you're happy. That's good.'

'Am I?' she teased, unconsciously flirting with him as she gave him a long look from under her dark eyelashes. 'How do you work that out?'

'Because time doesn't matter when you're happy.'

'Oh,' she breathed, and let the matter drop. She had to because he was smiling back at her in a way that said he was happy too, and the joy that spread through her effectively robbed her of speech. She finished her wine to give herself time to recover, and firmly refused another. She felt intoxicated enough.

She also felt too full to eat the banana concoction that was the final course, and nibbled her way through some freshly picked grapes while she waited for the men to finish. She felt mellow now as well as happy, and hoped that the mood would outlast the meal.

She needed Marcus's co-operation for that, of course, but he was still smilingly courteous as he led her and Jason from the dining- to the sitting-room. It was the first time she had been in here, and yet it was startlingly familiar.

It took her a moment to figure out why, and then she realised it was because it was full of the same deep sofas and armchairs as the house in Richmond, where comfort ruled over the fads of fashion. It also gave her the same cosy feeling of being at home, and she gave a deep sigh.

'There you go again,' Marcus said. 'Sighing those deep sighs that I don't like the sound of.'

'It's only contentment because I feel so much at home in this room,' she replied honestly.

'That I do like the sound of,' he approved, and went over to a drinks tray on a sideboard and lifted a decanter of brandy. 'Will you both join me?'

Sheona shook her head, and so did Jason, as he folded himself into an armchair close to one of the open french windows. Sheona wandered over to the mantelpiece and studied the silver-mounted family photographs displayed there.

The next thing she knew Marcus was standing beside her, his arm going around her waist as though it had a right to be there. He put his glass down on the mantelpiece and picked up an oval photograph. 'My father,' he said.

'I guessed. You're so like him.' Sheona picked up a matching frame and added, 'This must be your mother. She was very beautiful.'

'She would have been very upset at you rejecting her perfume without even trying it,' he murmured.

'Marcus, that's not fair! My reasons for not using it were nothing to do with your mother. I was just being——'

'Yes?'

'Bloody-minded,' she confessed, then blushed vividly.

Marcus laughed, and bent his handsome head to breathe in her ear, 'Do you know how adorable you are when you blush?'

'No, and I don't want to know,' she replied hastily, her fingers fumbling as she replaced the photograph of his mother and blindly picked up another. His breath on her ear was making her curl up inside, her nerve-endings transmitting seductive messages all over her susceptible body.

'Still can't accept compliments, can you?' he observed softly as he straightened up and moved slightly apart from her, much to her relief and regret.

She thought it better not to reply, concentrating instead on focusing on the photograph. 'Annabelle,' Marcus explained.

'But she's lovely!' Sheona exclaimed involuntarily, studying the wide dark eyes so like Marcus's and the far daintier, perfect features. 'Good heavens, she could give Shireen—and anyone else, for that matter—a run for her money! Are you quite sure you're right about——?'

She broke off, wishing fervently that she'd been less impulsive and more discreet. Now she'd raised one of the bones of contention between them, and she really hadn't meant to. She looked nervously up at Marcus's face, expecting his dark eyes to flash, his heavy frown to lower.

His expression had certainly altered, but not in the way she expected. He looked, if anything, uncertain— but that couldn't be right. Marcus was *never* uncertain. 'Don't let's quarrel,' she added quickly. 'It's been such a lovely meal, such a lovely evening, such——'

He put his fingers on her lips to still the rush of conciliatory words, and she longed to take his hand and kiss it and make peace between them again. Not, as it turned out, that it was necessary, because he said, 'We're not going to quarrel. We're not even going to talk about Annabelle or Shireen. Not tonight, not tomorrow, not until——'

It was his turn to break off, and she prompted, 'Not until...?'

'Well, not yet,' he answered awkwardly.

Marcus...uncertain *and* awkward. *Marcus!* What was going on?

Jason was obviously wondering the same thing because he stirred in his armchair and asked, 'What secrets are you talking over there?'

'I don't have any secrets,' Sheona answered slowly. 'Ask Marcus.'

Marcus, though, was clever enough to dodge the issue by saying teasingly, 'A woman with no secrets? That's something new, but perhaps it's time to decide what we're going to do with the rest of the evening? The moon's up. Does anybody fancy a walk along the beach?'

'I'm game,' Jason replied, standing up and rubbing his stomach reflectively. 'I think I've eaten too much. It'll do me good to walk it off.'

'Sheona?' Marcus asked as Jason went out on to the veranda.

'I think I'll call it a night. It's been all go over these past few days.' She was being perverse again, and she knew it, because there was nothing she wanted more than a moonlight walk along that perfect crescent of a beach with Marcus. She wanted to go so much that she wouldn't have cared if a dozen Jasons had accompanied them—but she was uneasy. Just as she'd thought she and Marcus had made their peace, another pit had yawned between them. A pit she was afraid to look into.

So far in their relationship they'd had plenty of mis-understandings, plenty of quarrels, but she'd always felt that Marcus had been honest with her. Now she wasn't so sure, and she was knocked sideways by the suspicion that he was deceiving her in some way.

But why should he? Why should an arrogant man like Marcus bother to stoop to deception when he had plenty of other sure-fire methods of getting what he wanted?

It was a puzzle, and, the more she thought about it, the more certain she became it existed only in her mind. She was so incredibly sensitive to Marcus that she was over-reacting again, and all because he'd hesitated when she was used to his being so sure. Heaven knew she hesitated enough herself!

'Would "please" make any difference?' Marcus asked.

'Pardon?' She stared at him, not understanding, so deep had she been in her disquieting thoughts.

'Would "please" tempt you to come for a walk? I'll carry you back if you get too tired.'

Sheona wavered, her heart at war with her head. Marcus held out his hand to her. She took it, unable to help herself.

Her heart had won.

*   *   *

Sheona lay in her bed some time later, staring up at the white filminess of the mosquito net. It made her feel she was in her own little world, and she didn't want to be in her own little world.

She wanted Marcus.

He wouldn't come to her. She knew that with certainty. Something had changed in their relationship. The kiss he'd given her on the cheek when he'd brought her up to her room after their walk had been positively chaste. Somewhere, somehow, she'd lost the brute who'd told her roughly that he could have her on the floor if he wanted her, and found a gentleman who gave her all the respect she craved.

Except that she hadn't—quite—wanted to lose the brute. Not altogether.

Sheona flung herself over and buried her face in the pillow. She couldn't cope with all the wild and wilful emotions seething inside her. She'd never experienced love, lust—whatever it was!—in such a violently explosive form. It frightened her, how close she was to losing control. What was worse, it excited her, too.

Not for the first time she told herself that this wasn't her, Sheona Murray. This was some creature Marcus had created. Only he could get her into this state. And only he could get her out of it.

Sheona blushed in the darkness, a blush that was no less painful because she was alone. She was still fighting the primitive side of her nature Marcus had exposed, still slightly ashamed of it. No wonder she could find no peace!

Why, oh, why did Shireen have to run away and start the chain of events that had got her into this mess? She'd been comfortable with herself and her life up until then. She certainly wasn't comfortable now.

Suddenly, for no good reason she could think of, she remembered the perfume she'd left on the veranda rail

before dinner. So what? she tried to tell herself. It was
perfectly safe out there, and even if it wasn't Marcus
probably had dozens of bottles. But she wanted the one
he had given her, and she wanted it now. It was a link
with him. A tenuous one, but still a link.

And she needed something of him! Then, perhaps,
she'd be able to sleep. Her white nightgown wasn't much
more substantial than the mosquito net she lifted to get
out of bed, so she slipped her arms through the matching
négligé.

That wasn't very substantial, either, but it made her
feel more respectable as she went softly towards the
french windows. She was a little nervous of the communal veranda, although everybody else must have fallen
asleep long ago.

She opened the windows and glided towards the veranda rail, breathing in the scents of the exotic flowers
down below in the garden, scents which seemed even
more potent in the still night air. She breathed in something else as well and half turned, staring along the veranda. She saw the glow of a cigar and tried to draw
back, but it was too late.

Marcus said out of the darkness, 'Don't run away,
Sheona. Come and talk to me.'

She knew then that it hadn't really been the bottle of
perfume she'd been seeking. It had been him. And now
that she'd found him she didn't know what to do. She
hesitated, then whispered, 'I'm—I'm—scarcely decent.'

'If you were stark naked you'd still be decent,' he replied. 'It's one of your special qualities—special because
it's so rare.'

Was that a compliment, or a polite way of saying he
didn't find her desirable? Sheona didn't know, but she
found the courage to say, even though it wasn't strictly
true, 'I came out here for a breath of air, not for a—
a—quick adventure.'

'A quick adventure,' he repeated, sounding amused. 'You have such a quaint way of putting things, Sheona, but it's all right: I'm not interested in a quick adventure, either.'

So he didn't desire her. She was safe. How ironic! It was Sheona Murray who wanted to be safe, not the restless creature within who had forced her out here tonight.

Feeling like two people uncomfortably sharing the same body, she walked towards him. The polished boards of the floor felt warm and smooth under her bare feet; strangely sensual. How conscious of everything she was tonight, how extraordinarily conscious. Like a wild animal whose survival depended on its awareness of its surroundings.

Marcus was sitting on the broad veranda rail, one leg sprawled casually along it, the other touching the floor, his back resting against one of the upright supports. The night had a dark, velvet quality but she had her night vision now and she could see he was naked but for shorts.

That made her throbbingly aware of the transparency of her lace nightgown and négligé, apart from the scraps of smooth satin insets. We shouldn't be here like this, she thought, although she also knew it was the hope of being here like this that had kept her wakeful.

'I'll get you a chair,' Marcus said.

'Don't bother,' she replied huskily, propping herself on the veranda rail a few feet from him and leaning back against another of the upright supports. She didn't feel embarrassed or ashamed any more. In fact, she almost felt that she and Marcus had shared the quiet of the night like this before... or would again.

He flicked his cigar away and Sheona followed the wide glowing arc until it hit the ground a few feet away from the house. 'I hope cigar smoke doesn't offend you,'

he said. 'I rarely touch them, but tonight I needed—
something. It's not often I can't sleep.'

'Me neither,' she replied softly. It was true enough—
until she'd met him, anyway. 'I suppose Jason is fast
asleep?'

'I'm not interested in Jason. Tell me about yourself.'

'You know everything there is to know about me.
Age—twenty-two. Profession—artist. Vital statics——'

'Not that sort of stuff. Tell me about the real you.
Your ambitions, your hopes, your dreams. I want to
know it all.'

'You'd be bored to tears. Apart from being a dead
ringer visually for my sensationally sexy sister, I'm too
ordinary for words.'

'Ordinary is the last thing you are. I thought I'd made
that perfectly clear already,' he replied with a flash of
irritation that rasped her nerves and reminded her forc-
ibly of the brute she'd been missing such a short time
ago.

Marcus recovered his calm immediately, though, and
continued more quietly, 'Do you see your parents often?'

'I spend Christmas and occasional weekends with them
in Winchester, and sometimes they come down to visit
me. They're very busy people. Mummy teaches art at a
polytechnic and Daddy's now the senior partner in his
firm of solicitors.'

'Were they disappointed that neither of their daughters
was interested in law?'

'No, they always said we owed them nothing except
being happy, if we could manage it. They're very nice
people.'

'They sound it.'

They talked on, and it wasn't until some time later
that Sheona realised she'd told Marcus all the things he
wanted to know about her, and that he didn't seem in
the least bit bored.

In fact, he was encouraging. 'I looked at your sketches while you were asleep this afternoon,' he said when she fell silent. 'They're very good. I'd like to commission some commemorative plaques of Drummond Island to sell to our tourists. They always want something to remind them of their holiday. Are you interested?'

'I'm interested,' she gasped, 'are you serious?'

'Very. Your work is original, distinctive and beautiful. I'm sure it won't be long before it's highly sought after by collectors. I'd like to get in on the ground floor, as it were.'

Sheona's cheeks glowed at his praise and she almost jumped off the veranda rail to hug him. She recollected herself just in time, but her delight was reflected in her exclamation, 'Is that your honest opinion? I mean, you're not just flattering me?'

'I wouldn't dare. I know how you feel about flattery, and I'm far too business-minded to land myself with a lot of china that doesn't sell.'

That Sheona could believe, and her delight increased. 'Marcus,' she breathed, 'Marcus, there are times when I almost...'

'Yes?' he asked intently.

'...like you,' she finished, overtaken by shyness again.

He was silent for a moment, then he replied drily, 'I'll try not to let your raptures go to my head.'

Sheona chuckled. Then she surprised them both by saying impulsively, 'It's more than "almost", Marcus. I do like you. I really do.'

Marcus stood up and came towards her, looming tall and powerful in the darkness. He lifted her down from the rail, his hands lingering on her bare arms. 'Then you'd better go to bed. Now, this second, or you won't be going anywhere at all.'

CHAPTER ELEVEN

MONDAY was one of those days marked out in Sheona's life to be special. She was aware of it first thing, when Marcus greeted her at the breakfast table with a smile that went straight to her heart. She felt he'd been waiting to see her again as much as she'd been waiting to see him.

Falling in love must be something like this, she thought, and for once she didn't recoil from the idea. She had no need to. Her senses told her she could stop being so suspicious and defensive. Whatever she was feeling, Marcus was feeling it, too.

She didn't know why she was so certain of that, only that she was. Somehow, somewhere, she and Marcus had developed a trust and respect for each other that was too honest to allow for deception.

She began to enjoy all the emotions that had formerly frightened her, feeling that they were at least being given the right encouragement to develop naturally. She and Marcus had been plunged into a situation neither had expected or been ready for, so that they were now going back to the beginning to rediscover each other.

If it had only been infatuation they would have jumped into bed together last night, and that would have been it. But that wasn't what Marcus had wanted, which was why she was so reassured and confident today.

Last night, after all her doubts, she'd discovered that he did desire her but, more importantly, that he was prepared to wait. It could only be because he was falling in love with her as heavily as she was with him.

Certainly, everything that happened during that blissful Monday pointed that way. They bathed, they dived, they lounged in the sun, they explored the island, never more than a fingertip away from each other.

All right, so Jason was with them as well, but that didn't matter. Both she and Marcus were behaving as though they had all the time in the world to enjoy the ever-deepening bond between them, and that was what made Sheona so confident, so happy.

'Chalk and cheese,' Jason muttered to her once when they were sunning on the beach and Marcus was searching for seashells for her. 'Who do you think you're kidding? You two have the hots for each other.'

For the first time she felt a flash of real annoyance towards him. 'You don't have to be so crude,' she snapped. 'It's not like that at all.'

Jason's blue eyes opened wide. 'You mean it's the real thing? Sorry, I didn't know it was like that.'

'It isn't like anything—yet—and that's why I don't want to talk about it,' Sheona replied, regretting her outburst. 'I'm sorry, too. I didn't mean to snap your head off.'

'Forget it,' he replied easily. 'Just send me a piece of the wedding-cake.'

She shoved his handsome head in the sand and fled towards Marcus for protection. 'What's the matter?' Marcus asked, catching her around the waist so that her body swung against his by its own momentum.

The contact made her more breathless than she already was, and she gasped, 'Nothing.'

'It had better not be,' he threatened, releasing her with reluctance. 'I'm the jealous type.'

She stored his words away among the other treasures of the day, to be remembered and smiled over during the long hours of the night—hours that came all too soon.

'Don't come out on the veranda tonight,' Marcus told her as he took her up to her room after dinner. 'What's between us is very special, and I don't want to grab at you, but that doesn't mean I won't if I'm given half a chance. Do you understand?'

'Yes,' she whispered. 'Oh, yes.'

'Then goodnight, my lovely captive. You'll never know how hard it is to be a decent gaoler!'

He kissed her full on the lips, and with a tenderness that made her want to weep. Then he left her.

When Sheona stared up at her mosquito net that night her eyes were like stars. Even her restless body found a kind of peace. She had experienced the searing flames of passion first, and now she was experiencing the soothing balm of romantic love. She fell asleep imagining what it would be like when the two came together, and when she awoke she was smiling.

It was a leisurely morning, a repeat of yesterday, and she seemed to be in a dream, but that was all right because it was a dream that Marcus shared.

At the back of her mind she knew that this was Tuesday and the leisurely pace of life on Drummond Island was about to change, but she lived each hour by the hour, shutting out everything but her ever-growing love for Marcus.

It was just after midday when she couldn't shut out the world any longer. The launch arrived, spilling out the amazing amount of specialists it took to make a commercial. The final duration might be less than a minute, but it was still like making a miniature film.

There were the production manager, the director, the video cameraman, the sound recordist, the lighting expert, the film editor, the make-up girl, a 'stills' photographer responsible for the poster shots—and five gorgeous models of varying nationalities.

'My harem,' Jason said.

'You mean for the video?' Sheona asked.

'Here's living in hopes it will be for more than that,' he grinned, going forward to help them on to the pier. 'It's a bit of a bind playing gooseberry to you and Marcus.'

Me and Marcus, she thought, hoping for a warming glow, but as all the video equipment was unloaded she was overcome by the all-too-familiar feeling of inadequacy. Like it or not—and she hated it!—she was face to face with the reason Marcus had brought her to Drummond Island.

She desperately needed reassurance, and if Marcus had been close she would have slipped her hand in his and not cared what anybody thought. But Marcus wasn't close. He was organising the transport of the film crew to the holiday village.

She felt abandoned at a time when she needed him most. That was unreasonable, of course, but it was impossible for her to be reasonable with so much nervous tension knifing through her.

They were all supposed to be lunching together in the thatched tourist restaurant, but Sheona had no appetite. She slipped away, driving one of the mini-mokes up to the house, where she collected her sketching materials and went out into the garden, settling down in the shade of a gracefully curving palm tree to draw a delicately perfumed frangipani bush.

Deep down she knew it was an attempt to hang on to herself in her own right, and not let herself be swallowed up again as an indifferent look-alike for Shireen. Time passed, as it always did when she was absorbed in her work, except this time part of her remained detached. Waiting...

'You're a bit anti-social, aren't you?'

Her busy pencil stilled. This was what she'd been waiting for. Marcus—and criticism. 'Yes,' she agreed, seeing no point in prevarication, 'but that shouldn't surprise you. You know how I feel about modelling. Any time a film crew's close I panic.'

'Even though you're just as lovely as Shireen, and have just as much to offer?' he questioned quietly.

'I can't tell you how many times that's been said to me before,' she replied, striving hard for calmness. 'It didn't work then, and it doesn't work now. I just hate modelling. There's nothing weird about that. Most people hate things they're no good at.'

'You've got me to help you through it this time. Don't you think that will make a difference?'

She turned towards him, her wretchedness reflected in her eyes. 'I don't know.'

'Will you try? Just for me? I've brought Tina, the make-up girl, and Frank, the stills photographer, up to the house. I thought if we took some poster shots with nobody else around it would help build up your confidence before we start shooting the video tomorrow.'

'You mean right now?' she asked, panic closing in on her.

'It's the best way. The longer you have to think about it, the more nervous you'll get.' Marcus closed her sketchbook and drew her to her feet. 'Trust me, Sheona,' he went on softly. 'I know what's best for you.'

Did he? she wondered, returning reluctantly to the house with him. 'I didn't think it would come to this,' she burst out as he led her upstairs to her room. 'I can't believe Shireen hasn't made any contact at all.'

Marcus hesitated, then said, 'As a matter of fact, she has. She'll be here on Thursday.'

'Thursday!' Sheona echoed. 'That's a day after shooting on the commercial starts. Where is she and what's happened to her?'

'I expect she'll explain all that when she gets here.'

'But—but...' Sheona protested, and then fell silent. If Shireen had, as Marcus suspected, been with his sister's boyfriend then naturally he wouldn't want to talk about it.

There was no time for any more private conversation because Tina was already in her room with her makeup kit open and waiting. Marcus gave Sheona a swift, reassuring kiss on the forehead before he left her, and that was all Sheona had to hang on to while Tina got to work.

Tina was in her late twenties and as London as Tower Bridge. She certainly knew her work. She also knew Shireen. 'Talk about two peas in a pod,' she said cheerfully. 'I'm blowed if I can tell you apart.'

'We're totally different in personality, Tina.'

'I've heard you're the quiet one.' Tina began to smooth cosmetics on Sheona's face, then fine them away, explaining cheerfully, 'Subtlety's the key for the natural look, but that's no news to you, is it? You were a child model.'

'I never liked it. That's why I got out.'

'So I've heard, but you've grown up now. You'll be able to cope better.'

It was a confidence Sheona was far from sharing as she put on the bikini Shireen had worn in the first commercial. She tried to imagine she'd also stepped into her sister's skin, but she couldn't. The old feeling of inadequacy was too powerful.

'Right, that's it,' Tina said, spraying Sheona liberally with Slave. 'You look and smell terrific. Shireen to the life.'

'But I'm not Shireen,' Sheona said desperately, her voice almost breaking.

'Don't worry about it, love,' Tina told her bracingly, as she repacked her make-up box and carried it to the door. 'If you can fool me you can fool anyone, even yourself. It'll be as easy as rolling off a log, you'll see. Jason's already made up, so we can get going.'

'I'll be right down,' Sheona promised, frozen to the spot as she fought off an attack of nerves.

Marcus came in as Tina went out. He was wearing cream shorts and a matching shirt with short sleeves, epaulettes and big patch pockets. He looked so masculine that she had to swallow hard, but it was a very woebegone face she turned towards him.

'Stage-fright,' she explained, trying to smile and failing miserably. 'I'm going to be dreadful, I know it. Oh, Marcus, surely you of all people understand that it takes more than looks to be a model? I don't know exactly what it takes—an inner glow, perhaps—but whatever it is, I haven't got it.'

'Yes, you have,' Marcus replied positively. 'You haven't realised it yet, but you will, and you'll be wonderful. Just tell yourself you're the most desirable girl in the world.'

'But I don't believe it!'

He took her trembling hands and held them firmly in his strong ones. 'I do,' he said, and bent his handsome head to kiss her on the neck, and she gasped as the sweetest of emotions quivered through her body.

'Do you believe me now?' he asked huskily.

Sheona wanted to so much...but another dreadful fear beset her. 'How do I know this isn't just another hype? You could be turning me on deliberately, just to get the result you want. That's what you did when we first met and you made it plain you'd do it again if you had to.'

Her breath caught in a little choke in her throat. Suddenly the relationship that had been developing between them, which had been going from strength to strength, became very fragile again. She didn't want to ruin it, she really didn't, but it was more than time that they were honest with each other. Images weren't good enough any more. She needed reality.

What if... dear lord... what if he'd been deliberately holding back so that he could really turn the heat on when the right moment came—right for him and his wretched commercials?

She swallowed hard and she forced herself to continue, 'If you're just coming on strong to me to get me ready for the camera it won't work. It will turn me off just as surely as the patter of a professional photographer. I'm just *incapable* of believing that sort of stuff.'

Marcus released her hands and took a step back from her. His lips twisted as he told her, 'You don't have to remind me what a brute I've been to you, or why you have such little reason to trust me. I'm only too aware of it.'

He unbuttoned one of the pockets on his shirt, drew out a slim sheaf of papers and gave it to her, saying, 'Your tickets home. They're for the launch, the local plane to Mahe and the jet to England. You can use them any time.'

Sheona stared at him wonderingly. 'M-Marcus,' she stammered, 'what does this mean?'

'That you're no longer my captive. You can leave any time you want.'

'Shireen?' she faltered.

'She won't suffer for it. The blackmail, kidnap—call it what you like—is over.'

'But—but your commercials.'

'I always try to get my priorities right,' he replied with a bitter smile. 'I thought I had them right when I brought you out here, but being with you has shown me how wrong I was. The truth is that you've become the most important thing in my life. That's why I can no longer force you to do anything you don't want to do.'

'Marcus...' she breathed, pure happiness bringing tears to her eyes and drowning all her fears. How could she doubt him any longer when he was prepared to keep an expensive film crew in idleness until Shireen returned? That just wasn't the sort of thing a hard-headed businessman would do—unless he cared more about her than money.

She went blindly into his arms and shuddered with delight as he caught and held her closely. She lifted her lips gladly and closed her eyes, joyful tears still seeping from under her closed eyelids as he kissed her. If she'd thought she'd known pure happiness before then this must be ecstasy, she thought deliriously as they drew apart and looked at each other.

It seemed to Sheona that everything they needed to know about each other was there in that look, and sudden shyness made her joke huskily, 'Are you sure this isn't just because I'm wearing Slave?'

'If that's what you think...' Marcus began fiercely, lowering his dark head to hers again.

He got no further because, after a cursory knock on the door, Jason came bounding into the room. He was wearing tight white trousers, a medallion, and nothing else but his bronzed skin. 'What's the hold-up?' he asked breezily, then stopped short as he saw them in each other's arms.

'Get lost,' Marcus growled, but Sheona smiled and shook her head.

'We'll be right down,' she promised, and as he grinned and shot back out of the door she took Marcus's beloved face in her hands and reminded him, 'We have some pictures to shoot, Marcus.'

'You don't have to do them.'

'I want to.' Sheona shuddered, but it was only with relief as she realised she meant what she said. She loved Marcus, so naturally she wanted to help him. 'I could face a whole battery of cameras now,' she told him. 'Just one will be a piece of cake.'

Marcus frowned and searched her eyes. 'If you're absolutely sure...'

'Let's do it.' She grabbed his hand and pulled him laughingly from the room. 'Right now, before Tina has to do a complete new job on my face instead of just a retouch.'

'You've never looked lovelier, my darling,' Marcus vowed.

'That's just your opinion—the camera's might be different. Tina's certainly will,' she teased, carried away by the euphoria of the moment. Was this really her, this laughing, vital creature who hadn't a care or a doubt in the world?

It must have been, for her confidence and euphoria lasted all through the photographic session. Frank, the photographer, posed her with one of the time-sculptured granite rocks on the beautiful crescent beach as a backdrop. White-edged turquoise wavelets lapped at her feet, and Jason, behind and slightly to one side, was instructed to look adoringly at her.

When Frank was satisfied with all that he concentrated his attention on her, and began the flattery that was his own particular hype. For once Sheona wasn't resentful. He had his job to do, and he did it the best way he knew how. She didn't disbelieve his fulsome flattery, either, because there was Marcus watching, his eyes confirming that everything she heard was true.

'Magnificent, Sheona! You're absolutely terrific! Now give me a raunchy pose. Legs farther apart, one hip jutting forward. No, no, the other hip. That's it. Stupendous! Breathe in, thrust those beautiful breasts out. Great! Now give me that smouldering look. Wow! Tremendous. Now...'

It went on and on while the instructions and the 'great's and 'terrific's flowed, and the camera clicked incessantly. Sheona wanted to be great, she wanted to be terrific, she wanted to be marvellous—for Marcus, but that didn't matter because it worked.

She felt none of the old inadequacy spreading its inhibiting tentacles throughout her body so that she froze into immobility. The way she felt for Marcus and, more importantly, the way he felt for her, had cured her of all that.

'Whoever said this twin was the dud?' Frank marvelled when he finally called a halt. 'She's as good as Shireen, and I never expected to say that of anyone.'

A little of Sheona's euphoria died. She didn't want to be as good as Shireen—she just wanted to be herself, the woman Marcus had made of her. She turned to him and said uncertainly, 'Marcus...?'

'I'm not comparing you,' he said quickly. 'You know I've never been confused about which twin you are, and which one's mine.'

Mine...

That was the one word she needed to know, and euphoria reclaimed her like a warm, reassuring blanket. She could trust Marcus, therefore she could trust her own feelings for him and not deny them any longer.

Except that she wasn't called upon to deny them. That evening she, Marcus and Jason dined with the film crew and the five lovely models in the holiday village. Sheona wore a white gown that was little more than a handful of white silk, and for the first time in her life she felt she had the power to fascinate that had always been Shireen's.

Sheona had never envied her for it, her natural shyness always making her prefer a background role. But then, she'd never been in love with a man like Marcus before, never felt the need to shine down the opposition. Now she welcomed her new-found confidence, a confidence that grew as Marcus stayed close by her side.

The dinner turned into something of a party, and Jason elected to stay when Marcus drove her back to the old plantation house. It looked magical in the moonlight, the scent of blossom heavy on the still night air.

Yet she was conscious of little but Marcus by her side as they went up to her room. She wanted him so much, and yet underneath this new Sheona he'd created she was still herself.

When he took her into his arms as she'd known he would she turned her face aside and said hesitantly, 'Marcus...'

'Yes?' he asked softly.

'Will you be mad if I say that none of this seems very real to me?'

'No, I won't be mad. However we feel, we've still known each other only a few days. That's what you mean, isn't it, what's bothering you...?'

'Yes,' she said gratefully. 'I—I'm just not the sort of person to—to...'

'Leap into bed at the drop of a hat,' he finished for her. 'I know that, too.'

'B-but when we first met you s-said you could have t-taken me on the f-floor if you'd w-wanted to,' she stammered, blushing fiercely.

'That hurt, didn't it?' he replied, caressing her cheeks with loving fingers as though to cool them. 'In fact, it hurt so much that you've never been able to forget it.'

'Yes.'

Her answer was little more than a sigh and he lowered his head to press a feather-light kiss on to her neck. 'I'm sorry. I said a lot of things I regret,' he murmured against her soft flesh, his warm breath playing havoc with her senses. Instinctively, quite unable to help herself, she nuzzled her head against his, all control slipping in the sensuality of the moment.

Marcus put his hand on her glossy hair, stroking it soothingly as he continued, 'I know it's going to take me time to live down the way I was, but try to understand I didn't like what I was doing to you. I *had* to be brutal to force myself to go through with it. I was expecting a different sort of girl, tougher, more resilient, but you were so sweet, so defenceless. I tried to kid myself you were putting on an act.'

He stopped, drew a deep breath, and went on, 'Now I know differently. You'll always be sweet and defenceless, and I wouldn't change you for the world.'

'Marcus,' she breathed. 'Oh, Marcus...'

He put her resolutely away from him. 'That's why it would be wrong of me to rush you, why I've been trying to keep control of the way I feel about you. It isn't easy, but your happiness is more important to me than anything else. When you're ready come to me. Then I'll know you've forgiven me, and that I'm not forcing you into another situation against your will. I've vowed never to do that again—ever.'

He brushed his lips tantalisingly across hers, and then he walked away. Sheona watched him stride along the passage and into his own room. She even watched the door close behind him, and she felt so bereft that she wished she'd kept her mouth shut.

She'd made Marcus think he still had to prove something to her, but he didn't, he didn't! She raised trembling fingers to her lips to try to quieten the storm of emotion he'd aroused in her, and failed abysmally.

Brute, bastard—whatever he'd been in the past no longer mattered—he was her darling now and she wanted him so much. His self-inflicted penitence was touching but it left her with a yearning to reassure him that was so fierce, so immediate that she wished she'd gambled everything on going heedlessly into his arms and to blazes with the consequences.

You're a fool, Sheona Murray, she told herself bitterly. Only you would look paradise in the face and worry about whether you're going to be kicked out of it or not.

She paced her room, back and forth, back and forth, and then in exasperation she had a shower. She towelled her glowing body dry and slipped on the most virginal nightie she had, its crisp white folds falling to her feet from a demure broderie anglaise bodice.

Still she felt as though she were on fire, and she was so conscious of Marcus's presence in the next bedroom that the thick dividing wall between them might not have existed. If only she could be as brazen as the image she'd created for the camera that afternoon, but she was incapable of carrying it over into real life. If Marcus were with her, perhaps, but he wasn't, nor was he going to be. Not tonight; not until she plucked up the courage to go to him of her own free will.

She had the will, all right, but not the resolution to back it up. However much she burned for him, she was still too shy. She needed *him* to take the initiative. Surely a man of his experience must know that? Hell, why had she hesitated? Why, why, why?

With a groan Sheona climbed into bed and lay in her white netting cocoon. Not long afterwards she climbed out again. She could find no peace, no rest.

The tropical island with its sense of isolation, its fiery sunsets, its scented air, its strange night calls of animals and insects she had no knowledge of seemed to have crept under her skin, making her a vibrant creature of the tropics, too.

No, not the island, she corrected herself disconsolately. It was its master that had done this to her. He was the one who was keeping her wakeful, discontented.

She wandered restlessly over to her dressing-table, switched on a side-lamp and studied herself.

How unlike herself she looked. Virginal, certainly, in her prissy nightie, but wild as well with her dark hair loose down her back, her brown eyes glowing and her lips parted in anticipation of something that wasn't going to happen.

She sighed and her glance fell on the bottle of Slave on the dressing-table. Marcus had made her part of its hype, and therefore she should be cynically immune to its promotional message. And yet her hand reached for the bottle, seeking the comfort of something he had touched.

She unscrewed the cap and lifted it to her nostrils. She breathed in the perfume that seemed to have something of the aura of the island in it, and she dabbed it on her skin and her hair. Then she wished she hadn't. It only made her more restless than ever.

The overhead fan was stirring the air incessantly, and yet she yearned for the freshness of a cool sea breeze. Then, perhaps, she'd be able to sleep. She opened the french windows cautiously and stood looking out to sea, breathing in the velvet balm of the night air. No smell of cigar smoke. She could go out on to the veranda without feeling like a brazen hussy.

She was one step away from the veranda rail when Marcus said, 'Sheona...'

She stood poised for flight but at the same time she knew she was never going to run away. This was what she'd been seeking all the time... Marcus! She'd just needed to fool herself with other reasons, other excuses for coming out here, that was all. It was the way she was.

She watched him come towards her, naked save for shorts that glowed whitely in the moonlight, and it was like watching a scene she'd already experienced in her dreams a thousand times before. Herself standing here like this, bathed, perfumed and waiting, and Marcus coming purposefully towards her.

He took her straight into his arms, waited for a fleeting moment to see whether she would pull away, and when she didn't drew her close against his almost-naked body. She sighed and leaned her head against his chest, a signal of surrender in what had always been a losing battle.

'Sheona...' Marcus breathed again, this time more raggedly, and then he kissed her with a tenderness that melted her body until it seemed to fuse with his. The kiss lasted for an eternity of bliss, and yet when it ended it was still too soon, leaving them both craving for more... and more.

Sheona felt love flowing between them like a powerful force nothing could stop, and when Marcus began to shower kisses all over her face she turned her head this way and that to kiss him, too.

Desire was mounting like an irresistible tide within her and she flung her head back to expose her neck and shoulders to his searching lips, her eyes closing as he found one vulnerable nerve-point after another.

She felt his fingers undoing the buttons of her demure bodice and held her breath as he pulled her nightgown apart and found her heavy breasts. She gasped as his hands covered them, exploring and massaging every soft inch until his fingers grasped her taut nipples.

Her hips swayed against his, unconsciously seeking to alleviate the desire raging through her like the sweetest of torments. She gasped again as she felt the hardness of his arousal, and then he caught her up in his arms, bending his dark head to clamp his mouth over one of her breasts as he carried her along the veranda and into his room.

His bed was huge, an antique four-poster hung with mosquito netting. When he placed her inside and lay beside her she felt they were truly in a world of their own. At last.

Then the sweet torment began again as he tenderly pulled her nightgown down to her feet, his lips following every inch of flesh he exposed, exploring, caressing, arousing. He threw her nightgown away and drew back to look at her in the soft moonlight.

'My sweet Sheona,' he murmured. 'My darling girl...'

Then his hands and lips began another exploration of her body, skilfully demanding now where they'd previously been tender. This was an entirely different assault upon her senses, and she reacted passionately, meeting his demands with demands of her own as her hands rampaged over his strong shoulders and muscled hips, and her lips pressed hot kisses on any part of his flesh she could reach.

'Marcus, for pity's sake...' she breathed as her desire built up into a crescendo he refused to satisfy. Then she understood his restraint, because he parted her silken thighs and caressed those secret parts of her no man had ever touched before. Her back arched and she writhed in torment until her passion peaked in an explosion of ecstasy.

Marcus reared over and into her, and she scarcely felt the pain of his first thrust in the reverberations of her own ecstasy. She clung to him, her eyelashes wet with joy as he claimed and made her his own. She never wanted this union to end, but, when Marcus gave a great cry and collapsed against her, she cradled him in her arms.

He pressed hot, damp kisses into her neck, raised himself to kiss her on the lips, then collapsed again. She held him lovingly, her lips smiling as their heartbeats slowly returned to normal, initiated now into a power she'd never known she possessed.

After a while they parted, lying side by side on the pillows and smiling at each other. 'Do you want a cigar?' she teased softly.

'I don't want a damn thing,' he growled. 'I've already got all I ever wanted...you.'

Sheona rolled towards him and sighed blissfully, her eyes closing. She felt Marcus's arms come around her and, snug in their security, she drifted off to sleep.

She wouldn't have slept so peacefully if she could have seen the way Marcus was frowning up at the canopy of the huge four-poster.

CHAPTER TWELVE

SOMEWHERE a telephone was ringing. Sheona stirred, but it seemed far away. Its insistence was just becoming important when it ceased. She sank gratefully back into sleep and remembered no more.

The golden light of morning was filling the room when she returned to consciousness. She was still very drowsy, reluctant to wake, and she turned instinctively towards Marcus.

He wasn't there.

Sheona sat up and blinked owlishly at the empty space beside her. It was a moment or two before she saw the note on his pillow. She reached for it and clutched the single sheet of paper anxiously.

Sheona, my love, forgive me for not being here when you awake, but Cordelia has been taken ill and I must return to England. I have so much to say to you but it will all have to wait until I get back. You were sleeping so sweetly that I didn't like to wake you. Meanwhile, remember you don't have to film if you don't want to. Marcus.

Cordelia...ill? Sheona felt a swift surge of compassion. She knew how devoted Marcus was to his second mother. She remembered now the ringing of the telephone. So it hadn't been part of a dream! Oh, if only he'd woken her! She wanted to share all of his life, the bad bits as well as the good. Surely, after last night, he realised that?

But no, it seemed she'd entered the small magic circle of those he wished to protect. Sighing, she retrieved her nightgown, struggled into it and got out of bed. She stood looking at the massive four-poster where she and Marcus had consummated their love, and touched the white netting with loving fingers before she returned regretfully to her own room.

She bathed and went downstairs for breakfast. The house scenes that featured in the next two videos were going to be shot today—except that she didn't have to do them if she didn't want to. She would, though. For Marcus.

It was very difficult without him there to draw strength and inspiration from, but she did her best. It took its toll, though, and by the time filming halted for lunch the tension had got to her. She felt like a wrung-out rag.

While the others went down to the tourist restaurant for their meal Sheona flopped on a sun-lounger in the garden, wondering how Cordelia was, where Marcus was now, and how she could get through the afternoon's filming without him.

She had no idea when she would see him again, but he would telephone, surely, as soon as he could? Sighing, she closed her eyes, trying to recapture the perfection of yesterday, her memories blurring into dreams as she dozed lightly.

She was shaken awake by excited hands, and a laughing voice exclaiming, 'Sheona, you rogue, you've finally learned how to switch on for the cameras! The film crew say you've been marvellous. Oh, wake up, love! I'm bursting to know how you've managed.'

Sheona opened her eyes and stared at her mirror image. 'Shireen! But—but you weren't supposed to get here until tomorrow!'

'I tried to obey Marcus's orders but I couldn't help getting anxious. I thought you might need some help, kiddo.'

'Do I ever! Oh, Shireen, I can't tell you how good it is to see you!' Sheona sat up and hugged her twin, then as she came fully awake she questioned, 'Marcus's orders? What orders?'

'To stay away until he'd coaxed some filming out of you. I must say he comes up with the most marvellous ideas, but that's why he's so successful, of course. Just think of all the publicity we'll get! Such a boost to my career, and surely yours as well, quite apart from helping to launch Slave. We're all on a winner, I tell you, thanks to him.'

A cold hard knot formed where Sheona's heart had been, and she asked, 'What idea, what publicity? Shireen, what are you talking about?'

Her twin perched herself on the side of the sun-lounger and grinned. 'Sorry, I was forgetting. You don't know anything about it, do you? Marcus said it was important you didn't, because you'd be bound to chicken out of filming if you knew I was available.'

She hugged Sheona again, and said, 'So *noble* of you, love, to step in to save my career, and I'll never forget it. Honest! Even though it wasn't necessary. I know how you hate cameras, but Marcus promised me faithfully that he'd let you off the hook if it got too much for you. But the film crew say you've beaten your old hang-ups and been fantastic. I'm so thrilled for you. Now you've made enough money to put that funny old house in Bournemouth straight, with some left over for a rainy day! Isn't it terrific?'

The chill that iced Sheona's heart began to spread along her veins, freezing her to the very marrow. 'Shireen,' she said haltingly, 'I still don't know what you're talking about.'

'I'm getting to it, darling. When I got to Mahe, naturally I phoned Marcus here right away, but he said——'

'When was this?' Sheona interjected.

'Sunday, love.'

Sunday! And Marcus hadn't said a word about it. Whenever she'd asked if Shireen had made contact he'd prevaricated—or lied. Marcus, whom she'd learned to love and trust!

'Anyway,' Shireen rattled on, 'he told me to check into whichever ritzy hotel I fancied and he'd pick up the bill, plus pay my normal fee, because of this marvellous idea he'd had. A spot-the-twin competition. He's going to put you on one of the posters, and in one of the scenes of the second and third commercials, and there'll be a huge prize for whoever can tell you apart from me. Just imagine all the extra public and media interest that will arouse! Slave can't fail. Isn't Marcus brilliant?'

'Yes,' Sheona replied, no warmth left anywhere within her. 'Quite brilliant.'

And I'm a fool, she thought bitterly. I believed in him. I trusted him. I thought he loved me, and all the time he was hyping me up to promote his wretched perfume. But he didn't have to carry his scheme all the way to bed, did he? I'll never forgive him for that. Never!

'Sheona,' Shireen said, her brilliant smile fading a little, 'you don't seem very pleased. I thought you'd be delighted to beat your camera jinx, and make some real cash into the bargain. Marcus kept his promise to let you go if your nerve failed, didn't he?'

'Oh, yes, he kept it,' Sheona assured her. And she'd taken it as proof of his love... when it had been no such thing!

'That's all right, then,' Shireen breathed, relaxing. 'For a moment there I thought——'

'Why did you vanish?' Sheona interrupted abruptly. 'Marcus thought you'd run off with his sister's boyfriend.'

'I know,' Shireen chuckled, 'but it was no such thing! Annabelle and I became really good friends when I stayed over at the Richmond house to discuss making the commercials with Marcus. Then, when we came out here to film the first one, Annabelle came with us. Mike Judson was holidaying here and they fell for each other. In a big way.'

'That much I know,' Sheona interjected. 'What happened after that?'

'Well, Mike's always been such a womaniser that Marcus thought he was just playing with Annabelle. He even made Annabelle doubt Mike, because she really looks up to Marcus. He's been as much a father as a brother to her, and the poor kid was so unhappy. So I cooked up a scheme with her to prove whether Mike was serious or not. You're going to love this, Sheona, it's a real lulu.'

'I'm sure I will,' Sheona replied, amazed at how normal she sounded when inside she felt dead. Absolutely dead.

'Yes, well, Annabelle's beautiful but Marcus has guarded her so well that she's a total innocent. She has no idea how to *use* her sex appeal. Me, now, I trade on it. So Annabelle and I figured that if Mike was only fooling with her I'd be able to charm him away if I really turned on the works. So I did, but Mike wasn't interested. I tell you, the way I threw myself at him he had to be in love with Annabelle to resist me!'

'Marcus was wild about that,' Sheona replied quietly. 'He—he thought Annabelle's obsession with Mike would burn itself out if you'd left well alone.'

'That's because Marcus doesn't know anything about love,' Shireen retorted, knocking the final nail in the coffin of all Sheona's hopes. No, she thought, all Marcus knows about is opportunism—using people. As he used me.

'Anyway,' Shireen continued, 'when the filming was over Mike and Annabelle were desperate for some time together without Marcus interfering. That was pretty nigh impossible, or it would have been if I hadn't pretended to run off with Mike.'

'So that's the way it was,' Sheona mused. 'I didn't think it was like you to steal Mike away from Annabelle just for kicks.'

'Of course it wasn't,' Shireen scoffed, 'but Marcus wasn't to know that. He only knows me professionally, not personally.'

That careless piece of information would have been balm to Sheona's aching heart if it hadn't been for all the rest, but nothing—nothing!—would ever be able to soothe her now.

'To shred a long story into digestible parts,' Shireen went on irrepressibly, 'Mike and I flew to the Bahamas while Annabelle flew to England. When she was supposed to return to university she flew out to join us. You'd have thought they'd been apart for centuries! It was love all right, the marrying kind. So they got married!'

'Then you flew to Mahe,' Sheona finished for her.

'After I'd been bridesmaid at their wedding! That's why I couldn't meet my contractual agreement with Marcus. I sent my SOS through you so that he wouldn't have a clue where I was.'

'He knows all this now?'

'Sure. I told him on Sunday, but Annabelle had just phoned him herself.'

'How did he take it?'

'Amazingly well, considering. I suppose it helped that Mike's going to buy a place close to Oxford so that Annabelle can continue her studies.'

'Where are they now?'

'On honeymoon. It has to be short because he's supposed to be recording, and she's supposed to be studying.' Shireen pushed back the heavy hair that had fallen across her face, and sighed, 'And that's about all my news. How are things with you?'

'Fine,' Sheona lied.

Shireen looked closely at her and asked, 'Are you sure?'

Sheona thought she might—just!—hold herself together for a little while longer if nobody discovered what a fool she'd been over Marcus. Her hurt was so deep, so raw that she couldn't even bear to talk of it to her twin.

But, somehow, Shireen was already suspicious, and to allay her suspicions Sheona replied with what she hoped sounded like a burst of candour, 'Well, it's been—interesting—here but the truth is that I'm pretty desperate to get home. I—I—had some heavy commitments of my own to fulfil when Marcus hauled me out here. I won't be really happy until I'm just an artist again.'

'It's not been hell, has it?' Shireen asked, alarmed.

'No,' Sheona replied, and she wasn't altogether lying. Some of it had been paradise. Hadn't she always known deep down, though, that it couldn't last? Wasn't that what all her doubts had been about? Those doubts that Marcus, damn him, had overcome so skilfully? To stop her twin questioning her too closely she said, 'I suppose the film crew told you Marcus had to fly back to England because Cordelia is ill?'

'Yes. Isn't it awful? She's such a honey, too. There's no news, I suppose?'

'No, Marcus won't even be in England yet.' A thought struck Sheona and she said, 'Shireen, how did you get here?'

'I met this lovely old couple who were cruising round the islands on their yacht, and hitched a lift. They have a honeymoon every ten years, and this is their fourth. Isn't that sweet?'

'Yes,' Sheona replied automatically, her mind on other things. 'Then the regular launch hasn't called in yet?'

'Not as far as I know.'

Sheona swung her legs off the sun-lounger. 'Great, so if I pack fast I should be able to get on to an island where I can get a flight to Mahe.'

'What's the rush?' Shireen asked, dismayed. 'I thought we'd at least be able to spend a day or two together.'

'I understood about your work, can't you understand about mine?' Sheona pleaded. 'We'll have a big reunion and gossip when you get back home.'

'Yes, sure, but——'

'Then come and help me. We'll have to be quick, not least because——' Sheona consulted her watch hurriedly '—you'll have to be before the cameras in half an hour.'

She'd struck exactly the right chord, because Shireen stopped expostulating. It was Sheona who threw things randomly into her case while Shireen showered and shampooed her hair ready for a filming session. The twins hugged quickly, and Sheona said awkwardly, 'Shireen, when Marcus phones don't tell him I've left, will you? Fob him off somehow.'

'Why?' her twin asked, puzzled.

Sheona didn't want him knowing she was in England while he was there in case he tracked her down again. It wasn't likely, but she didn't want to take any chances. The thought of seeing him again before she'd pulled herself together made her frantic.

'Why?' Shireen persisted.

Somehow Sheona managed a smile. 'Just in case he gets another promotional idea to drag me back here. As far as filming's concerned I've had it for the time being. He's—he's not likely to understand that, but you do, don't you?'

'Sure I do,' Shireen replied, tightening her hug.

Sheona smiled mistily at her, then she was flying down the stairs, leaping into a mini-moke and driving down to the pier. She had no time for any farewells, and she didn't regret them because her control was already stretched to breaking-point.

The launch had already made its daily deliveries and was set to depart when she hurried aboard it. She was its only passenger, so there was nobody she had to make small talk to.

It was the only thing she had to be grateful about that day.

Two days had passed since she'd fled Drummond Island. Sheona sat in her studio on Friday evening trying to recapture the peace and contentment that had been hers before Marcus had stormed into her life. It was useless.

She'd gone over and over it all a thousand times until her head ached as much as her heart, and the conclusion she came to was always the same.

Marcus had used her.

With all his professional expertise and personal charm he'd projected a personal image to bend her to his will...and she, gullible fool that she was, had made it easy for him.

He should market himself, she thought bitterly. He'd make a mint.

But that he should have had the nerve to leave a note that began, 'Sheona, my love...'!

Her eyes filled with tears. She blinked them away. Marcus wasn't worth weeping over, even if her heart thought that he was.

She looked at the coagulating paints on her palette. She picked up her brush, then put it down again. It was no use. She'd tried—she'd tried really hard!—to work, but deep down she'd known that she was never going to.

It was only an excuse to shut herself away from her housemate, Petra, who was watching television in the sitting-room.

This need for isolation, which had first shown itself when she'd been incapable of explaining to Shireen exactly what had happened between herself and Marcus, was the one thing within her that seemed to be growing while everything else was withering. She knew it was bad, and yet she couldn't do anything about it.

All her life she'd preferred to lick her wounds in private. Other wounds healed, though. These Marcus had inflicted on her just grew worse.

Once more she had to fight back the tears, and once more she succeeded. More or less. In the background she could hear the dramatic soundtrack of some old film Petra was watching, but she deliberately shut it out. Pain was a strange thing. At least, the sort of pain she was suffering was. All-absorbing, impatient of distractions.

Like her love for Marcus.

Sheona groaned and buried her head in her hands. She heard the doorbell peal but it didn't matter. Petra believed she was trying to catch up on neglected work, and was under strict orders to make sure she wasn't disturbed.

She could trust Petra. That was one thing in a topsy-turvy world that hadn't changed.

Sheona believed that, right up until she heard a certain firm footstep outside her studio and the door burst open with a crash.

Marcus!

She knew it even before she jumped up from her desk and turned to face him. There he stood, tall, powerful, and so soul-destroyingly irresistible. And yet he looked different. He was unshaven and his ruggedly handsome face was drawn with weariness.

Even while she was drumming up her hate for him she was concerned at the way he looked. As though he hadn't slept or rested for days.

Behind him Petra was saying, 'I'm sorry, Sheona, but he just pushed past me! Shall I call the police?'

'Call the fire brigade if you like but it won't make any difference,' Marcus growled. 'I'm going to talk to Sheona if I have to barricade us in.'

'Well!' Petra exclaimed, her indignant eyes meeting Sheona's questioningly.

After a moment's indecision Sheona shook her head. She knew Marcus well enough not to doubt that he meant what he said. She just couldn't understand what he was doing here, though, or why he looked so—so shattered.

'It's all right, Petra.' She was surprised to hear herself sound so unruffled, so normal, when all the time she was almost suffocating from Marcus's dominant presence in her studio.

'If you say so,' Petra replied, unconvinced. 'I'll only be in the kitchen. Shout if you need me.'

The door shut behind her. 'She sounds like a good friend,' Marcus said unexpectedly. 'I'm glad about that. I haven't been much of a friend to you, have I?'

'I thought your object was to be my lover. You were pretty good at that, as I recall,' she retorted icily.

'Ah, Sheona...' he breathed, and held out his arms to her.

She retreated behind her chair, her rejection of his invitation so blatant that his arms dropped uselessly to his sides. 'What's the matter?' she asked. 'Is it Cordelia?'

'She's all right,' he replied quietly. 'She was rushed to hospital with a suspected heart attack, but it was nothing so serious. She's been overdoing things and just needs to rest.'

'I'm glad.' She was, too. Cordelia was such a warm, totally natural person that it was impossible not to care what happened to her. 'Now you've told me that, there's nothing else you can say that I'd be remotely interested in,' she continued distantly.

'Don't give me that,' Marcus retorted roughly, taking a step towards her. 'You and I haven't even begun to talk yet, and you know it.'

Sheona couldn't retreat any further, so she stood her ground, hoping she looked a lot braver than she felt. She certainly sounded dignified as she said, 'Marcus, I can't force you to leave. I can only ask you. Just for once in your life do the right thing, and go away.'

'No!'

The word seemed wrung out of him and the next thing Sheona knew he'd thrown aside the chair between them and grasped her in his arms. He pulled her against the long, hard length of his body and buried his face in her hair. 'I can't go away,' he muttered thickly. 'You're mine, and I'm not leaving without you.'

With a superhuman effort Sheona held herself stiff and unyielding in his arms. 'I'm not yours,' she denied hotly. 'You never loved me, Marcus. You used me. I hate you for it. Do you hear me? I hate you!'

She tried to tear herself free but his arms were like iron bands around her, and the more she struggled, the tighter they closed. 'For heaven's sake, give me a chance to explain,' he begged.

'Explain!' she mocked bitterly. 'There's no need. I understand it all too well already. You wove a web of lies and deceit to put personal pressure on me for your own professional gain. I'll say one thing for you, Marcus—you're certainly dedicated to your work. You even put in a bit of overtime in bed!'

'Stop it,' he said, shaking her. 'It wasn't like that. If you'll just listen for a minute——'

'Spare me the fairy-story,' she scoffed breathlessly. 'Make a commercial out of it. It might sell a few million more bottles of perfume.'

'Stop it!' he thundered. 'Stop being so damned cynical. Be the girl I fell in love with. My sweet Sheona.'

'Your stupid Sheona,' she retorted, twice as incensed that he should dare to say he loved her, 'but I've wised up. You're never going to take me in again.'

'I'm not trying to take you in. I'm trying to tell you that I love you!' he raged.

He almost sounded as though he meant it. For a second Sheona's heart stopped, then better sense prevailed. 'You don't know anything about love,' she snapped. 'Love is trusting. Love is respecting. Love is caring. Love is...oh, all the things you know nothing about!'

'Then why the hell do you think I'm here? Since Wednesday I've flown to England, back to Drummond Island, then straight back to England again because you'd run away from me. I'm out on my feet, Sheona, but I'm here—because that's where you are. Doesn't that tell you *anything?*'

'Only that you've got some new trick up your sleeve that I don't want to hear about.'

Marcus shook her again, this time much more fiercely. 'It should tell you that I love you, woman! Everything I've done since I met you has been because I loved you. Can't you see that?'

'No, I can't,' she flared. 'All I can see is how you lied and cheated, and manipulated me for your own ends. Am I now expected to believe you did all that because you loved me?'

'Yes, dammit, because it's the truth.' The fire seemed to go out of him and with a groan he pulled her into his arms, burying his face back in her hair.

He sounded so beat, so exhausted that Sheona impulsively raised her hand to stroke his dark head, and only at the last second realised what she was doing. She let her hand fall by her side, hating the instinct that made her want to comfort him when she was so much in need of comfort herself.

Much more quietly, with a sigh that seemed to come from his soul, Marcus went on, 'I fell in love with you so fast and so hard that I couldn't believe it, couldn't even admit it to myself. I'm thirty-two years old, for goodness' sake. It had never happened to me before, so I didn't trust it—or you, either. I'm not used to being...vulnerable.'

He broke off and a shudder ran through him. 'It's bloody awful, being vulnerable. I hated it. Now, I guess, I've got used to it. It's all part of loving, isn't it?'

Sheona didn't answer, but within her some unquenchable spark of hope fired to fresh life. She tried to smother it, be strong and safe again, and yet Marcus sounded as though he'd experienced the agony she'd been going through. Hard as she tried, she couldn't quite suppress a responsive quiver that made her tremble in his arms.

Marcus wrapped her more closely to him, but tenderly this time. After a moment he continued, 'My way of coping with finding myself vulnerable was by distrusting what I was feeling. In spite of that, I couldn't let you go. I just couldn't! So I came up with the "Spot the Twin" promotional idea. It gave me a perfectly valid business reason for keeping you close by me—a clear case of self-deception, my darling, while I got used to the idea of being in love with you.'

She felt his lips press into her neck and her heart began to beat like a wild thing again. More than ever did she want to stroke his dark hair, but still she checked herself. She'd suffered too much, and she was too dreadfully afraid of suffering again.

'I know it meant deceiving you as well,' Marcus went on. 'I justified it by convincing myself it was good for you to overcome your terror of the cameras. You see, I knew that once you were properly motivated you'd be every bit as good as Shireen, but I wanted you to know it, too, so that you'd never, ever feel like the "dud" twin again. I was trying to clear a shadow out of your life and I succeeded. I hope that counts for something against all the rest.'

'Why didn't you tell me all this before—before...?' Sheona's voice broke off in another choke.

'Before we slept together? I meant to. I truly did. But the trust between us was so precarious that I was terrified of losing you altogether. I needed time to prove my love to you, but Cordelia was taken ill and Shireen returned early and—and I lost you. I have to get you back, Sheona. I just can't live without you.'

Could she believe him? She wanted to. Oh, how she wanted to! But some things still hurt too much to forget. 'Shireen said she made you promise you wouldn't force me to film, but when you gave me those tickets and said I wasn't your captive any more you made it seem as though it were your own idea.'

'By that time I was so deeply in love with you that whatever I had or hadn't promised no longer mattered. I had to free you because your happiness meant more to me than anything else. It still does, and it always will.'

'Then . . . then . . . if I asked you to go you'd walk out of here and never bother me again?' she asked tremulously.

'No,' he replied, setting his jaw. 'When I walk out of here you're coming with me.'

That wasn't the answer she was expecting and she exclaimed, 'What kind of loving is that?'

'My kind of loving,' Marcus growled, turning her face up to his. 'It doesn't have a rule book. All it knows is that you and I belong together, no matter what.'

'You mean whether I like it or not!'

'You'll like it,' he assured her. 'I mean to spend the rest of my life making damn sure that you do.'

She should have stayed indignant—outraged!—and she knew it. But Marcus had his own way of doing things, and that was something she had to accept, along with the rest of the man. If she still wanted him . . .

'I—I thought you'd just used me,' she faltered. 'I thought that somehow I'd become only a part of an image you'd created to promote your—your . . .'

'This is no image,' he breathed, pressing urgent kisses on her eyes, her cheeks, her throat. 'This is the reality of my love for you. It even made me realise what a brute I'd been to Annabelle when I mocked Mike's love for her. I'd never experienced it myself, you see, so I didn't believe it existed. I do now.'

He shuddered, then went on, 'I even understand what crazy, irrational things love makes people do. All the wrong things, sometimes, because feelings don't exactly help the head to think straight. Will you forgive me? I'll make you forget the way I've been——'

'No,' she murmured, 'I don't want to forget. I want to remember it all, the good and the bad, because that's—us, isn't it?'

'Sheona, my sweet love,' he breathed, and kissed her upturned lips. A sigh shuddered through both of them, a sigh that banished the pain and healed the hurt. Marcus kissed her again and asked, his lips against hers, 'Are you coming with me, or do I have to carry you?'

'That's giving me about as much choice as you've ever given me,' she protested, but unconvincingly. 'Where are we going?'

'Does it matter?'

'No,' she replied, and it didn't. Not as long as they were together.

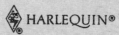

1993

The most romantic day of the year is here! Escape into the exquisite world of love with MY VALENTINE 1993. What better way to celebrate Valentine's Day than with this very romantic, sensuous collection of four original short stories, written by some of Harlequin's most popular authors.

ANNE STUART
JUDITH ARNOLD
ANNE McALLISTER
LINDA RANDALL WISDOM

THIS VALENTINE'S DAY, DISCOVER ROMANCE
WITH MY VALENTINE 1993

Available in February wherever Harlequin Books are sold.   VAL93

COME FOR A VISIT—TEXAS-STYLE!

Where do you find hot Texas nights, smooth Texas charm and dangerously sexy cowboys? CRYSTAL CREEK!

This March, join us for a year in Crystal Creek...where power and influence live in the land, and in the hands of one family determined to nourish old Texas fortunes and to forge new Texas futures.

CRYSTAL CREEK reverberates with the exciting rhythm of Texas. Each story features the rugged individuals who live and love in the Lone Star State. And each one ends with the same invitation...

Y'ALL COME BACK...REAL SOON!

Watch for this exciting saga of a unique Texas family in March, wherever Harlequin Books are sold.

CC-G

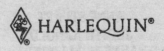

HARLEQUIN®

WELCOME TO

The quintessential small town,
where everyone knows everybody else!

Each book set in Tyler is a self-contained love story; together,
the twelve novels stitch the fabric of the community.

"The small town warmth and friendliness shine through."
Rendezvous

Join your friends in Tyler for the twelfth book,
LOVEKNOT by Marisa Carroll, available in February.

*Does Alyssa Baron really hold the key to Margaret's death?
Will Alyssa and Edward consummate the romance they began more than
thirty years ago?*

GREAT READING...GREAT SAVINGS...AND A
FABULOUS FREE GIFT!

With Tyler you can receive a fabulous gift, ABSOLUTELY FREE,
by collecting proofs-of-purchase found in each Tyler book.
And use our special Tyler coupons to save on your next
TYLER book purchase.

ROMANCE IS A YEARLONG EVENT!

Celebrate the most romantic day of the year with MY VALENTINE! (February)

CRYSTAL CREEK
When you come for a visit Texas-style, you won't want to leave! (March)

Celebrate the joy, excitement and adjustment that comes with being JUST MARRIED! (April)

Go back in time and discover the West as it was meant to be . . . UNTAMED— Maverick Hearts! (July)

LINGERING SHADOWS
New York Times bestselling author Penny Jordan brings you her latest blockbuster. Don't miss it! (August)

BACK BY POPULAR DEMAND!!!
Calloway Corners, involving stories of four sisters coping with family, business and romance! (September)

FRIENDS, FAMILIES, LOVERS
Join us for these heartwarming love stories that evoke memories of family and friends. (October)

Capture the magic and romance of Christmas past with HARLEQUIN HISTORICAL CHRISTMAS STORIES! (November)

WATCH FOR FURTHER DETAILS IN ALL HARLEQUIN BOOKS!

CALEND

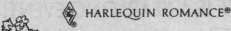

HARLEQUIN ROMANCE®

**Harlequin Romance
takes you to Alaska
for a wedding!**

Join us there
when you read
next month's title in

THE BRIDAL COLLECTION

**A BRIDE FOR RANSOM (#3251)
by Renee Roszel**

THE BRIDE wasn't looking for a husband.
THE GROOM didn't want a wife.
BUT THE WEDDING was right for both of them!

Available this month in
The Bridal Collection:
SHOWDOWN!
by Ruth Jean Dale
Harlequin Romance #3242

Wherever Harlequin Books are sold.   WED-10